This filly was

Everything in Dallas wanted to resist Jimi, but as he stared down into her upturned eyes, he saw something in them. Passion. Excitement. Vulnerability. And something he couldn't quite put his finger on, but he needed to find out what it was. Screw his rules. He'd rather be screwing her.

Jimi looked up at him and laughed, a deep, seductive sound that flowed under his skin, running like hot lava about to erupt.

"Anything to hog-tie and get you into bed, cowboy."

"No beds here—not fancy ones anyway. Just plain old cots."

She glanced at the cot and then back at him with a sexy grin. "I'm flexible."

"Now, that leaves room for interpretation, doesn't it?"

He continued to stare into her eyes as he lowered his face to hers. He lost himself in the feel of her. The taste of her lips on his and the sweet scent of her that seemed to surround him.

How many times had they kissed today? For strangers, they were doing pretty damn good.

And he wasn't about to waste any time with her.

Aloha, Dear Reader,

We're back in Hawaii! This time with a story of two completely opposite people. Jimi and Dallas come from very different backgrounds, or do they? How on earth will these night-and-day lovers ever make it work? Funny how a holiday romance can make you second-guess everything you hold most dear.

Hawaii is wonderful and I'm thrilled it is a setting for another story. This time we're on the Big Island. You'll visit numerous places along the way as Jimi and Dallas start their whirlwind love affair. But can they work out their differences? What about when the past is dredged up for Dallas and he has to make a choice? Oh, it's all so exciting! And Grant and Lana, from *A Taste of Paradise*, show up for a visit, too.

I hope you enjoy your trip back to the island and fall in love with Jimi and Dallas as much as I did. Their chemistry is smoking hot, and no amount of rain from a hurricane can dampen their flames.

Mahalo!

Shana

Shana Gray

—

A Cowboy in Paradise

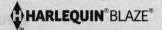

Recycling programs
for this product may
not exist in your area.

ISBN-13: 978-0-373-79960-2

A Cowboy in Paradise

Printed in U.S.A.

Shana Gray is a contemporary and erotic romance author. First published in 2010, Shana has written for Harlequin, Headline Eternal Romance, Random House Loveswept, Sybarite Seductions, Lyrical Press (now Kensington) and Ellora's Cave. Her scorching stories range from quickie length to longer romance novels. Her passion is to enjoy life. She loves to travel and see the world, be with family and friends, and experience the beauty that surrounds us. Many of her experiences find their way into her books. Visit her online at shanagray.com or at Twitter.com/shanagray_ and on Facebook.

Books by Shana Gray

Harlequin Blaze

"More Than a Fling" in *A Taste of Paradise*

Acknowledgments

Page Lambert and Amy Wight for helping me find just the right Western word.

Lisa Gibson Brijeski for being a great beta reader.

Deb Markanton for all the Hawaii info and making me drool with the photos. She's also a fabulous sounding board.

And thank you to the staff at the Four Seasons Resort Hualalai, Big Island, Hawaii, for your help.

Jenny Bullough for sparking an idea that found its way into this story.

Dedication

To my dad, Henry. He read *A Taste of Paradise* and I wish he was still here to read *A Cowboy in Paradise*. He passed away July 23, 2016, and has found his own ever-after paradise with Mom. Love you both always, xoxox.

_1_

JIMI CALLOWAY COULDN'T comprehend a destination wedding in Hawaii that wasn't on a beach. The wedding was inland. On a ranch! No beach in sight. Her words echoed in her ears. _Please just take care of the arrangements. Tell me when I have to be at the airport_, she'd told Jose, her assistant, when the invitation had arrived a couple of months ago. Now she wished she'd not been so damn preoccupied with the finishing touches to her first commissioned gown for the Oscars and paid more attention to the finer details of _this_ event.

Jimi sweated under the hot Hawaiian sun. Raising her face to the sky, she closed her eyes and absorbed the sun's energy. It was a whole lot better than dreary, gray and cold New York City. She got bumped from behind and nearly toppled off her Christian Louboutins.

"Oh, pardon me," Jimi said, and scampered not to sprawl into the dirt.

"My apologies." A heavyset man in a straw hat and

tropical flowered shirt steadied her by grabbing hold of her elbow.

Jimi gently pulled from his grasp. "It's okay. No problem," she said, smiling at him.

She glanced down at her Chanel dress. It had held up pretty well until now, after the twelve-hour flight and the bus ride from the airport to this Hawaiian ranch. She swept her hand over the fabric—covered in dust and travel wrinkled—finally giving up when her sweaty palms smudged the dirt. Shit, her hair would be 1980s huge in this humidity. Trying to blow the damp tendrils out of her eyes, she watched the luxury coach drive away, stranding her in the boonies of the Big Island. She'd had enough of the farm life growing up on a commune. Jimi shivered—a time she didn't particularly want to remember.

And to top it all off, her suitcase was lost. Panic began to set in. How would she face the day without the suitcase that housed her full armor of makeup, clothing and essentials? A habit she'd started years ago, she couldn't recall the last time she'd gone without makeup. Why hadn't Diana chosen the Four Seasons to have her wedding instead of here? Jimi swung her gaze back to the lady ranch hand who had delivered the upsetting news about her suitcase. Out of habit, she eyed the young woman all decked out in cowgirl clothes. The cowgirl looked at Jimi with clear gray eyes and confidence. Jimi bet she didn't have a worry in the world. She seemed so amazingly comfortable that Jimi almost envied her. The woman shifted her feet and spurs jangled in the dust. Jimi glanced down at the impressively tooled creations.

"Wow, I love your cowboy boots."

"Thank you."

They were great boots, with turquoise leather inlay and stitching. Jimi looked up and met the young woman's eyes, doing her best to not let aggravation over her lost bag ruin the day.

"I'm really sorry about your suitcase."

"It's not your fault. I'm just thrown a little off-kilter by all this," Jimi admitted.

"I understand, but I'm sure it will arrive soon. My name is Larson and I'll definitely keep an eye out for your bag."

Jimi nodded, trying not to let her disappointment show. She'd been looking forward to unwinding in Hawaii after the wedding. It was a treasured bit of time between moments of chaos. She *so* needed to decompress. Vacation time that had been almost impossible to carve out of her busy schedule, but she managed and had lived for these precious weeks in Hawaii. Twenty-one days of sleeping in, relaxing in a cabana by the pool or beach, spa treatments and hopefully a bit of man time.

She'd been without a man's touch for far too long and desperately needed some attention from the male species. She'd been so busy and the promise to design Diana's dress was fit it in between the other orders. It was a beautiful creation.

Diana's dress! It was lost over the Pacific. In her suitcase. How would she ever explain this to her friend?

"Aloha, folks! Welcome to Broken Creek Guest Ranch!"

Jimi spun around, startled by the loud voice, which resonated in her chest like a loud bass drum. Deep, masculine and surprisingly seductive, it held a mild twang that completely caught her attention. Lost bags, Diana's dress and wrong destination momentarily forgotten, Jimi sucked in a breath as she pinned her eyes on the owner of said voice. Struck dumb, she hadn't expected to see such a hot cowboy. But of course there would be cowboys, right alongside cows, horses, flies and shit— a crazy mix next to the tropical foliage, beautiful blue skies and gorgeous flowers.

Hello, Hawaiian Hottie!

Jimi couldn't stop staring at the man standing on the front porch of the rustic-looking building. His head almost brushed the overhang he was so tall. She'd never been so drawn at first glance to a man before; he oozed a dangerous sexuality that reached across the dusty ground and lit her like a sparkler. He. Was. Gorgeous. It was like he snagged her with a lasso and yanked it tight. Jimi caught her breath and placed her hand over her heart as it tripped into double time.

This Hawaiian cowboy was large, muscled and tanned. He had it all going on. She smiled when she noticed the collar of his Western-style shirt. The pattern on the fabric was a ring of deep red hibiscus flowers. Only here could he get away with that. Her mind tumbled over itself as she considered ways she might be able to get this devilishly sexy cowboy on his own. Had a silver lining just appeared on the clouds of doom?

Jimi crossed her arms and hugged herself to keep from trembling, unable to drag her gaze away from him. She wasn't opposed to a holiday fling—preferably at a five-star hotel with butlers, vintage wine and gourmet dining and not on a ranch. Finally being able to afford the finer things, she'd become accustomed to them. Something told her this smoking-hot cowboy would transplant well and be a sweet distraction. *As long as he showered.*

She nodded to herself. She'd be able to make do for a short time without her bag. Seeing this delectable male specimen made her realize how travel weary she must look. The urge to step behind the cowgirl to hide herself made her shuffle backward without looking away from him.

His gaze swung through the crowd as he continued with his welcome. Then his attention fell on her. Jimi's feet froze and she was rooted to the spot—as if the dirt reached up and grabbed her ankles. Good Lord, he was too gorgeous for words. All Jimi's thoughts fled when a big, wide smile curved on his tanned face. He was clean shaven, but his dark hair was long, ruffling over his shoulders. Her belly fluttered—something she'd not experienced in…oh, ever. Unable to see his eyes, shadowed by the brim of his hat, made him all that much more enigmatic. She wanted him. Bad.

Her blood rushed and her arousal for him nearly made her swoon. She held her breath, enjoying the rare sensation as desire swept through her. The sun came out from behind a cloud, and Jimi raised her hand to shield her eyes from the glare so she could see him.

He seemed to be looking directly at her and she smiled. Did he smile at her? His gaze lingered a little bit and then moved on. The break in their connection was surprisingly disappointing.

"There's some grub waiting for you in the dining

room, and once y'all fill your bellies the luggage will be in the change rooms."

He pointed and she turned to the beautiful log building with paned windows and a wide front porch. Rocking chairs sat at the ready and there were even hitching posts and water troughs. Just like in classic Western movies. "There you can get on your riding gear while your horses are saddled and then we'll make our way—"

"Um, excuse me." Jimi raised her hand and waggled her fingers. "Did you say horses?" she blurted.

The cowboy placed a booted foot on the mounting block. Yes, she'd ridden and knew the lingo. She'd been a fairly decent rider, having grown up with horses on the commune, but fashion and makeup were her escape from that into a new and exciting world. Far from her impoverished growing up. His smile widened and he pushed his hat back on his forehead with his thumb. He leaned over and rested his forearm on his knee. She watched every move he made. Utterly mesmerized. His jeans tightened nicely over his thighs and hips. A flash of silver at his waist drew her attention to the monstrosity of a belt buckle and her gaze drifted lower until she realized she was gaping at his—

"You got that right, ma'am."

Jimi pulled her gaze away from his tempting bulge to his face and felt a flush grow on her cheeks. Had he caught her staring at his very manly package? She nearly groaned at the possibility and glanced around feeling uncomfortable that everyone was now staring at her like she'd grown a second head. She braced herself, expecting laughter to explode around her. Seemed it didn't matter how old you were—the insecurities from child-hood could rush back at the most inopportune moment.

Squaring her shoulders, Jimi turned back to the cow-boy. "I'm sorry, but I'm here for the McCain Scott wed-ding?"

"You're in the right place."

Her heart sank. "But this is for a destination wedding." Jimi waved her hand, indicating the miles of meadows beyond the very neat and tidy buildings. "There's n-no beach." She felt her cheeks flush hotter at the scattered laughter behind her. She wished the ground would break open and swallow her up.

"We have a beach on the property, ma'am. It's just a long way away from here." Not only was his drawl sexy and deep, she heard a compassion in his voice that made her feel a tiny bit better.

"S-so, no beach wedding?" she said, and immedi-ately wished she'd not asked the inane question which, of course, she already knew the answer to.

He shook his head and smiled again at her. He was totally charming and sincere, giving no hint he was making fun of her. Jimi relaxed somewhat at his calm tone. "Not right now, no."

She clamped her mouth shut, determined not to ask any more dumb questions. God, she'd really made a mess of things. If only she'd handled the arrangements herself, not passing them off. All she knew was the wedding was in Hawaii, with most arrangements made by the bride and groom. Guests provided their details, booked their own flights and hotel for after the wed-ding, with the suggestion of staying at the Four Seasons.

"In about an hour we'll ride up to the camp. Your luggage will be in the tents when you get there." He stood and hooked his thumbs into the pockets of his jeans. "Enjoy your meal and we'll gather at the barn across the yard."

Ride, tents? Jimi nearly screeched with building frustration but bit her lip. Panicked, she looked around at the other guests, clearly the only one who thought this whole trip to a Hawaiian ranch was a bad idea. The silver lining of only moments before had suddenly turned very dark and stormy.

She wanted to bolt right back down the road they'd just driven up but, seeing the dust settle from the long-gone bus, knew that wasn't going to happen anytime soon. Desperation overwhelmed her and she had to fight back the dread starting to set in. When tears sprang to her eyes, she was horrified. Jimi blinked furiously to stop any tear leakage that would further embarrass her not to mention smudge her mascara. She had to be here, though, for Diana.

Jimi straightened her back and drew in a shaky breath. She had no idea how she was going to face Diana or make do without any clothes, toiletries and the like. Somehow, she'd just have to man up. Surely there would be some kind of shop here where she could get the basics until her bag arrived. Fuck.

DALLAS WAS AT home in the saddle, and he was happy with the posse of wedding guests riding behind him. He'd never get enough of seeing all the excited faces when they stepped off the bus. It didn't matter how many years he'd been doing this, it never got old. Sharing his love of Hawaii, his ranch and all aspects of it was what he'd been born for. The Wilde family had been running this spread for over a century. Dallas looked at it as being a custodian of the land, honoring it as best he could. A caretaker. He was proud of his heritage and he'd encouraged his father and siblings to open their ranch to the public, to share with others. He hadn't been wrong and their business of eco-camping had really taken flight. Only this trip wasn't eco-camping. It was glamping. He shook his head ruefully. Glamping, of all things!

He thought of the blonde woman. She didn't fit the normal Broken Creek guest profile. When he'd first laid eyes on her he'd nearly forgotten his memorized speech. The wind had blown her hair across her face and she'd swept it away with slender fingers. Elegance had oozed from her and he could hardly imagine her holidaying at a ranch let alone riding a horse. That aside, he'd checked her out, from the tip of her sunny blond head, down her lean and fit body to her long and shapely legs, which he'd love to have wrapped around his hips.

No way would she be able to sit a horse in that tight sheath of a dress. But, Lord, he appreciated how fine she looked in it. And just like that he had a hankering to see that body naked. His groin tightened imagining her standing before him with nothing on but those killer shoes. He'd never seen such a razor heel and could almost feel the sharp stab of them in his ass as if she were under him as he banged her.

Those shoes were the damned sexiest things he'd seen in the longest time and a complete contradiction to the boots and runners on the other ladies around her.

All guests were told to bring shoes or boots with heels. This siren had certainly got that wrong in such a right way, and he knew he had to defuse this growing spark of interest. She looked every bit the prima donna.

And he made a point of keeping the divas at a good distance.

But, still, this one mystified him. She oozed a sensuality that made his cock sit up and take notice and elegance he shied from. A poor fit for the likes of him and totally not suitable for a rough-and-tumble interlude. Now the sensuality part…that was a whole other kettle of fish. She had a frosty exterior that made him wonder if in bed she'd be just as chilly or as sizzling hot as the Hawaiian sun. Dallas felt a flash of disappointment that he wouldn't be finding out the answer to that.

Best he steer clear of this tempting woman, even though every cell in his body wanted to try to melt this glacial filly. She spelled high maintenance and was not worth the trouble. Not his type. At. All. But, shit, he wanted a taste of her.

A shout from behind snapped him out of the rabbit hole he'd just fallen down. Dallas twisted in his saddle, scanned down the line of riders to make sure everyone was still doing fine. The wranglers would follow up the rear, so he wasn't too worried about losing anyone. But having forty guests was a little out of his comfort zone. Matt, the groom, was an old university friend. It surprised the hell out of him that his fiancée had agreed to a ranch wedding. He'd never met her but had heard stories about her. Girls' weekend away in Vegas. Jetting off to Bahamas and Paris. So this didn't really fit the persona he'd assumed for her.

Dallas huffed to himself, still not convinced marriage was the right thing to do. At least for him. Especially after being jilted at the altar. No sirree. Maybe, he reckoned, if kids were involved. But it seemed rather pointless to enter into a commitment that likely would bust up before long. He could count on one hand the number of marriages that had gone past the three-year mark. Anyway, he'd do whatever it took to make Matt and Diana's wedding day dreams come true. Even if he didn't believe in happily-ever-after. Women wanted to change a man to their liking, not accept him for who he was. Unlike men, who only want women to accept them for who they are and not try to change them.

"Another half hour and we'll be there," Dallas shouted, and bit back a smile at the chorus of groans.

Diana was insistent about comfort for the guests. Which meant he had to upscale all the prospector tents to a more *glamping* style. He shook his head, not understanding that at all.

The grove of trees beyond a wide, rolling meadow wasn't far-off. He liked it there with the pretty waterfall ringed by ancient and craggy lava rock. He'd chosen it especially for the camp as it was a protected location should extreme weather blow in. He sighed and wished they were there already so he could get the group settled and let the wedding planner take over.

Dallas patted Sweeny's neck. "I'll take you over a group of uncomfortable wedding guests any day." As if the horse knew what he said, Sweeny tossed her head, nickered in agreement and pranced sideways like they were the hottest couple in town. He chuckled and let her have her little moment of play. He'd be retiring her after this trip and breeding her.

He ran his fingers through her mane and hoped that she'd throw a good foal that would mature into a horse just as fine as she. Unlike the mare he was waiting on to foal anytime now. She was a Thoroughbred and covered by American Prince, a Triple Crown winner and Dallas's step into the racing world on the mainland. He was determined to give it a try, regardless of the chiding remarks his siblings made. He could handle it, mostly by ignoring them. It would take dedication and money to make it a go, money he'd worked hard to save. He didn't know a woman who wanted anything to do with the racing world. Fine thing, too, since he didn't need any added complications.

He hadn't entertained the idea of a committed relationship since…well, he'd rather not think of *her*. She'd soured him. Long since over her now, he'd learned a valuable lesson from that experience. Women were selfish creatures and told you what you wanted to hear before snagging you. Then expected you to put their wants and needs first. He hadn't met a woman yet who was willing to compromise and be a true partner. Sure, he'd dated, had a few flings and been hounded, too, but he was a confirmed bachelor, and he was pretty sure there was no woman who could make him consider otherwise.

Dallas looked up at the sky. Sunset wasn't too far off and he'd hoped to have all the guests bedded down in time for them to watch from Sunset Ridge while the

BBQ was prepared. No luau tonight—they were saving that for the wedding feast. Horsetail clouds winged in the sky, foretelling a change in weather. He furrowed his brows. Nothing significant had shown up on the radar last he checked, but that could change at the drop of a hat here on the island. The sky spoke to him better than any sort of technology. And it was telling him a different story. Storm coming.

Stress knotted at the back of his neck, but he refused to consider the possibility of weather ruining the wedding trip. He wouldn't say anything to the happy couple yet. Tomorrow was a riding trip to the beach, which made him think of the blonde woman—and his cock told him it was just as eager to see her prancing on the sand in a bikini as he was—then the wedding party rehearsal in the evening. The next day a wedding breakfast for everyone, and the ceremony in the afternoon with an evening luau only to ride back down the following day. Seemed like a colossal waste of time to him, but it was revenue in the bank for them.

He pulled Sweeny up in front of the river and called to the riders behind him. "This is our last crossing, folks. Remember to keep moving through the water and don't let your horse get his head down."

Sweeny stepped into the water with no need for Dallas to cluck her. She knew the drill. The water ran belly deep under the horses, slow moving and crystal clear. He hoped they didn't get surprised by any rain over the next three days; otherwise, it would make things mighty difficult.

2

Jimi did her best to keep calm even if she was roaring inside with frustration. She chewed on her finger and stared at the clothes generously donated by the other guests. She truly was thankful and would make sure she said so later. Looking forlornly around the tent that would be hers for the next three nights, Jimi fought back tears and breathed deeply. She had no idea what Diana was thinking, having a wedding here. Jimi hadn't been in a tent since she'd left the commune when she was of age.

Sorting through the clothes, she picked out a shirt and jeans that looked like they might fit. The plaid shirt and jeans would be way too big. The strip of baling twine would have to work as a belt. Holy hell, she felt like Elly May Clampett, and might as well just put her hair up in pigtails.

She opened her purse and fingered her compact, afraid to look at herself. But she did and gasped. How would she ever get through this week without her makeup kit, moisturizer and hair products? *But it wasn't the end of the world, right?* She'd been an earthy girl before, and she could give it a whirl again.

Jimi stared wistfully at her Louboutins, tossed aside when she'd kicked them off. They certainly looked out of place on the rustic wooden floor.

She shrugged off her dress, now almost beyond saving, and stood in her bra and panties. Jimi sighed as the fresh breeze blew through the tent, cooling her heated skin. The air smelled wonderful. Clean, crisp, fragrant and with a tinge of coolness that was a relief from the heat. She almost felt her stress and upset seeping out of her body, slowly rolling down her legs, over her feet and into the floor. Almost as if the ground sucked the negative energy out of her. She eyed the boots she'd been given, not wanting to put them on. It felt too good going barefoot, and she wiggled her toes when a rush of childhood memories came at her. Jimi distracted herself, refusing to remember.

A rustle outside the tent made her jump and she spun around. Jimi's heart nearly burst out of her chest when she saw standing at her tent opening the drop-dead-sexy cowboy from earlier. She couldn't read the expression on his face, but his mouth seemed to tighten and his eyes were heavy with an intensity that made her belly clench. He didn't look away from her. Instead, he met her gaze, then looked her up and down. More than once. She felt the heat in his stare as if he'd branded her. His searing look sent her body into turmoil, and her knees wobbled.

Jimi froze. It wasn't that she couldn't move—she

didn't want to. She tingled under his hooded gaze, feeling vulnerable, exposed and, yes, terribly excited. If she moved she might break this magically erotic moment. There was something about this man that made her want to throw caution to the wind.

Jimi wanted to say something witty and charming, enticing, but found her mouth suddenly dry and her tongue stuck to the back of her teeth. "Ah…" She cleared her throat. "Um…"

He touched his fingers to his hat and nodded. "I apologize, ma'am." His deep voice did all sorts of naughty sensual teasing to her senses. She wanted him to keep talking, this cowboy who had completely caught her in his ropes.

Jimi shook her head and stepped toward him, totally forgetting she was close to naked. "It's fi—"

She nearly stumbled when he walked toward her tent and placed a foot on the step in front of the raised floor. Then he filled the opening. *Was he coming in? Oh, God, please do!* He leaned in and reached to the side, yanking on a strap that released the tent flap she'd totally forgotten to drop down. He didn't let it fall right away, holding it for a few moments, his eyes never leaving hers.

Jimi melted. She felt her nipples rise against the lacy material of her bra, sending all sorts of wake-up signals straight down to her clitoris. She didn't give one whit that his eyes flickered down to her breasts before snaring hers again. Suddenly she wanted this man with a yearning that made her heart quicken.

The silence stretched. He seemed to loom bigger in the doorway, dwarfing everything else around him.

Jimi hadn't realized just how large and muscled he was when he'd spoken earlier. Now, close enough for her to take only a few steps and be able to fall into his arms, she trembled as his presence filled the little tent. Lord, she wanted to be wrapped in the strength of those big, powerful arms. The animal magnetism of this man had her ready to step off her very straight, narrow path and fall right into the tangle of the dark jungle.

"Ma'am. Remember to close the tent, keep unwanted critters out." And he gave her a crooked smile.

Then he dropped the tent flap and was gone, leaving her breathless and feeling empty. Jimi didn't move, now feeling utterly foolish, realizing she'd been in sight for anyone to see had they walked by her tent. Plus, she'd just stood there, close to naked in front of a strange, albeit very sexy, man. What must he think? She quickly pulled on the plaid shirt. Embarrassment rushed through her, followed by anger that she'd been placed in this frustratingly dumb situation in the first place.

DALLAS COULDN'T BELIEVE his eyes. A vision like that wasn't something you saw every day. He'd grown used to the daily ritual of horses, ranch hands and mountains. In all the years he'd been running the guest ranch, never had he walked by a tent to see a near naked and fantastically gorgeous woman. He'd watched her for only a few moments. Just long enough for his cock to sit up and take notice, and make him feel like a Peeping Tom. Hell, could you blame a man? Standing in her lacy and very sheer ivory bra and panties for all the world to see was totally unexpected. He was captivated.

He couldn't look away from her, like a lioness ready to pounce. Her blond curls fell wild around her shoulders and down her back. His fingers twitched with the urge to bury his fingers in the silky strands. Her almost virginal image oozed an untamed sexuality that reached deep down inside and grabbed him by the balls. Her smoking-hot body was anything but virginal—made for pleasure. And he'd be at the front of the line if given the opportunity. Shit, hadn't he told himself she was untouchable and for a few very good reasons? One being a risky business fraternizing with guests. It took a few minutes to gather his wits before he could move and react in a gentlemanly fashion. Dropping the tent flap had been his salvation before he'd stalked off to check the horses. A fine excuse to try to rid his mind of the imprint she'd made on it and his dick wanting something that likely would never happen.

Dallas sucked in a breath and knew it was no use. The image of her would be seared into his memory for the rest of his days. He also knew the only way he stood a chance to get her out of his blood was to bang her. But his gut told him that would only whet his appetite, making him want her more.

He entered the barn and wandered down the center between the horses. Their wide standing stalls either side of him ran the length of the shed row. Dallas had had the structure built a few years back to house up to fifty horses and storage for a couple hundred bales of hay. The peaked roof and no sides kept the weather and sun out, but the breeze from the ocean flowed freely. He'd also had storm shutters built into the roof that could be dropped down easily. He hoped like hell they wouldn't be needed on this trip. All the horses faced in, so it was easy to feed and water them.

"Hey, boss. We're all set," John said, tossing a few more flakes of hay into the last couple of stalls. He'd finished bedding down the horses for the night.

Dallas rechecked the ties and rubbed the forehead of every horse he walked by on his way to John. He loved the comforting sounds of their contented munching and their earthy scent. He loved everything about horses.

"Good job. Everything for the wedding all ready?"

"I guess so. I'm steering clear of all that hullabaloo. It's chaos, I tell ya, and I want no part of it."

Dallas laughed and nodded. "I'm with you there, buddy. Listen, keep it all tight, though. I have a feeling we'll be getting some rain."

John walked out from under the gabled roof and looked to the sky. "Ya think? Only thing that showed up on radar was about three hundred miles offshore, tropical-storm status but not heading this way."

Dallas nodded. "Still, keep an eye on the sky. A little bit of rain won't hurt anybody, but if that storm shifts and intensifies we'll be stuck up here."

John grunted his agreement as he walked away and said over his shoulder, "Time to get that barbecue fired up. Oh, hey, Tucker wanted me to tell you he was heading up."

Dallas nodded. His brother usually joined them, but wasn't sure if he'd be on island soon enough. He was also friends with Matt, and did his damnedest to get chickenshit Matt to surf. Now Diana had put a com-

plete stop to that activity, saying it was far too dangerous. Dallas shook his head and was glad he'd managed
to sidestep any long-term commitments where women
were concerned.

He lingered with the horses. They were his spirit animal and he felt best when hanging with them. He was
here as a wedding guest as well, not just as a boss or
ranch owner, but it was hard to not oversee everything.
All these people up here were his responsibility in the
long run and he wanted them to have the best time in
order for them to spread the word about Broken Creek
and bring in new business.

"Excuse me."

Dallas paused, his hand on the forehead of the gray
gelding. Both he and the horse turned in unison toward
the female voice.

Dallas sensed who it was. His heart thumped in his
chest like a smitten boy, which he was none too happy
about. The woman who only moments before had stood
close to naked in her tent walked toward him, her fingers tucked into her jeans front pocket. They were way
too big for her, and so was the plaid shirt. He noticed
she had bare feet. He raised his eyebrows, not expecting to see bare toes. But he liked it—maybe she wasn't
so high maintenance after all. It definitely made her
much more intriguing even though he didn't want to
be intrigued. Or tempted.

Her tits jiggled under the top. *Was she still wearing
that see-through bra?* Even with the baggy jeans and
baler twine for a belt, her curves left little to the imagination. Her hips moved with an enticing sway that made

him want to grab them and haul her up tight to him. Heat boiled down into his balls and he shifted his feet.

"Yes, hello." It was about all he could muster up with the images of her luscious body still seared into his brain.

She cocked her thumb behind her and gave him a direct look. "Um, back there. I—"

"Don't worry." Dallas shook his head, not wanting her to feel…what? Bad. Uncomfortable. Exposed. Yet he was so glad he'd walked by to get that visual treat. He'd been celibate far too long.

"I'm not worried. It's just that, well, if you liked what you saw, why didn't you just come inside?"

She was direct.

He narrowed his eyes and searched her face. Did she want a fling? Weren't wedding hookups commonplace? If she was offering, he decided he didn't want to let her down. That wasn't gentlemanly, right? But then who said he was a gentleman. He'd been told as much by… He refused to finish that thought and pressed his lips together. Ranch rules. *His* rules. No getting involved with guests. "Well, ma'am—"

"Please don't call me that. My name is Jimi." And she smiled at him, a seductive and enchanting curve on her lips that heated his blood. It was like the sun came out and shone down just on her, while everything else faded to black. He was mesmerized, again. Oh yeah, she spelled *trouble* with a capital *T*. Perhaps this would be a much more interesting weekend than he'd anticipated. He knew he was about to break all his hard-and-fast rules, which made him angry at himself just as much as it excited him. Something about this chick had his radar humming, and he was obligated to find out why.

"Pleased to meet you, Jimi." He offered his hand. She took it. Dallas was surprised by the strength of her slender fingers and the sizzle of erotic heat that flashed up his arm. He curled his hand around hers and pulled her ever so slightly closer to him. She didn't resist.

He looked down at her. She wasn't short, likely around five-seven, but still much shorter than his six foot two. He liked taller women, and her height was just under his preference. Still, though, he figured they'd fit together perfectly, just like puzzle pieces.

She gazed up at him and goddamn if he didn't lose his breath. Like Kilauea had erupted inside him. His blood pumped in his veins, hot, thick and achingly slow. He was lost in her eyes, which sparkled like stars twinkling against the indigo canvas of a Hawaiian night, a beautiful blue with tinges of amber and sand in their depths. Her curly hair a halo around her head. Dallas sucked in a breath as desire slipped down his spine and settled in his hips. In the short space of time since this woman had crashed into his life, it was like everything had changed. Something in his world had shifted. All he wanted to do was drag her into his arms, kiss her senseless and crush her to him. Dallas was rocked to the core, never before having had such a powerful reaction to a woman. All because of a smile, the touch of hands and a body he'd like to feed off for days.

3

JIMI STOOD IN front of this mountain of man, staring
up at him as he glowered down at her with an intensity that made her shiver. Her mind went nuts with the
possibilities of all the good bad things they could do
together. Something about this man made her want to
be bad. Naughty. While not a prude about sex by any
stretch of the imagination, it just wasn't often that her
body made the decision before her brain did.

His calm silence couldn't hide the passion she saw
brewing in his eyes. She wondered if he would be just as
intense and quiet if they fucked. Yes, that was how she'd
look at it. Not making love, no way. Love was something she'd given up on a long time ago. Anyone she'd
ever loved had left her. But that hadn't stopped her from
searching for it—God, how she'd searched—and in all
the wrong places, too. To distance herself from the un-
orthodox way she was raised had been her driving force.
She'd navigated through the concrete jungle of New York
City's fashion world and made it. At times, though, her

past came back to haunt her, like it seemed to be doing here, today. So many little reminders. It was unsettling.

She didn't feel guilty for seeking out men she could influence, manage to her liking. It meant she didn't have to let her guard down. It was purely physical. No entanglements. No talks of the future. Just the present. She'd learned long ago that the only person she could trust and count on was herself.

Jimi eyed this bad boy in front of her. He clearly fell into the physical-satisfaction category, and for a moment she wondered if he would be putty in her hands. His gentlemanly nature wasn't something she was accustomed to and would likely be his weakness.

"What kind of name is Jimi?" His deep and velvety voice captivated her. It held a hint of *cowboy* twang, which she liked.

"My parents were old hippies, commune types. They had a thing for Jimi Hendrix."

"Is that so? Then I expect you had the most unusual upbringing."

Jimi couldn't believe she'd told him that, and without any thought at all. It just tumbled out of her mouth. Usually she gave a bullshit story that they named her Benjamina and never ever said her parents were hippies. That usually led to all kinds of questions that she refused to answer. But he zeroed right in on what she needed to hide the most. Her upbringing and fallout from it. Surprisingly, he didn't inquire further or say anything more, and she hoped to quell any future questions.

"To say the least. Something that I try to forget."

He nodded and glanced down at her feet. "I guess some things are hard to leave behind."

She furrowed her brows and wondered what he was talking about, until she looked down at her bare toes. No way would she admit he was right. She'd buried her feelings deep where her childhood was concerned, but it seemed some things were hard to shake. "No. It's something I have most definitely left behind. My suitcase didn't arrive with me, so I'm at a loss for footwear other than my heels. Which appear to be completely inappropriate for this wedding trip."

"Ah, you're the one."

Jimi furrowed her brows. "What do you mean?"

"The one with no bags. The one that thought this destination wedding was at a beach. I barely recognized you."

Now he was making fun of her. She let go of his hand and was struck by the odd emptiness and feeling of distance that replaced the zing she'd felt from him just moments ago. The warmth of his fingers gone, a shiver ran through her even with the Hawaiian heat pressing down on them. She frowned, not liking how off balance he'd suddenly made her feel.

"It was my fault for not paying more attention. The norm for destination weddings is usually on the beach. At a resort. The last thing I'd expect here is a destination wedding on a ranch." She waved her hand to indicate her surroundings and nearly smacked one of the horses on the nose. The horse snorted and tossed his head, startling Jimi. She jumped and let out a cry when her bare feet landed on sharp stones, making her stumble.

She used the opportunity and in that moment decided to go with stepping up her game. So she let herself fall headlong into the cowboy. "Ow."

She was confident he'd catch her. She expected no less from this gentlemanly cowboy.

"Hey there, whoa."

She clutched at his arms, trying not to notice the strength under her fingers. At the same time, he wrapped his arms around her. Tight.

Regardless of whether she'd instigated this little event, she really had hurt her foot.

"Oh, my God, it feels like my foot shredded on glass." Yet the pain in her feet paled with the powerful response she had to him as he gathered her close.

"Exactly why you shouldn't be trotting around here without shoes on. Regardless if you're a hipster or not."

"I'm not a hipster! All right…enough. My feet are crying." The cowboy swung her into his arms. "Hey! What are you doing?"

"Taking you to fix your foot."

Jimi halfheartedly struggled in his arms, but the way she fit against his wide chest was far too comfortable. And wasn't it just where she wanted to be? Her foot was stinging, but the warmth of his body almost had her forgetting about it. "You know I'm quite capable of getting to my tent."

"I'm sure you are. But I don't need you leaving the scent of blood everywhere. Besides, the cuts will get full of dirt."

He took a path behind the rows of tents. She was glad he kept out of sight of other guests, because she already felt stupid enough with her dumb comments earlier. Jimi decided to just enjoy being carried. It wasn't every day a girl was in strong, muscular arms. She looped her hand behind his neck. His hair tickled her knuckles and she looked up, seeing under the wide brim of his cowboy hat for the first time. She swallowed when he looked down at her. All thought and words vanished under the heat of his gaze. And when he smiled—oh, God, when he smiled—she liquefied inside. What had she been thinking? No way would he ever be putty in her hands. Jimi feared it was *she* who would be putty in *his* hands.

He shouldered his way through a tent flap and Jimi glanced around. "This isn't my tent."

"I know." He set her down on a cot that looked surprisingly cozy and was very comfortable.

"Why am I here? I wanted to go to my tent." She was grappling with her rioting emotions, and being carried by him had thrown her totally off balance.

He pulled a chair in front of her, then turned around to a chest-high cabinet. "Does your tent have the first-aid kit?"

"Oh. I could have washed my foot off well enough," she argued rather unconvincingly.

"I'm sure you could've. But somehow you leapt into my arms, so I figured you wanted me to take care of things."

"I did not leap into your arms!"

"Could've fooled me."

Why did she feel defensive? Right from the minute she'd laid eyes on him hours ago up until now he'd had her completely off-kilter.

"Lift your foot," he instructed.

She did and watched in fascination as he cradled her heel in his big, tanned hands. He was so gentle as he tended her.

"Is it bad?" If it was, part of her hoped she might have to head back down for stitches. The other part wasn't so sure. He took off his hat and set it beside her on the bed, so close to her fingers that she touched the brim. A thrill ran through her. It was almost like touching a part of him. Almost.

He raised her foot a little higher and peered underneath. His dark hair appeared longer without his hat, and when he tipped his head, a strand fell across his forehead.

"Nope. Just a little cut. Nothing a Band-Aid and antiseptic won't take care of." He looked up at her and she drew in a breath.

He had the most intriguing eyes. Neither was the same color, but a myriad of sea greens in one, and arctic blues in the other. Jimi leaned forward slightly, as if magnetized to him.

"Your eyes."

"What about them?" He held her foot a little tighter.

"They're beautiful."

Jimi was surprised when he burst out laughing. The deep booming sound filled the tent and she blinked. What was so funny?

"They're just eyes, *hemahema*."

"But so unique."

"I can thank my mother for them." His smile was

wide, and Jimi saw his Hawaiian ancestry in the bold and strong features, dark hair and deeply tanned skin.

"Was she Hawaiian?"

"My grandfather was. Now, let's get this foot cleaned up."

"What's *hemahema*?" Jimi asked. "You said that a couple minutes ago."

"Clumsy, awkward."

"Humph. Nice."

He chuckled and then spoke in a low voice she could barely hear. "Your clumsiness got you in my arms, though. Didn't it?"

He glanced at her from under his dark eyebrows and her world tilted. The corner of his mouth lifted on one side and she was enchanted. That simple, seductive glance was full of so many promises. Promises she had every intention of making him keep.

"Yes, it did," Jimi whispered. "And I don't even know your name."

"Shall we keep it a mystery?"

Jimi gave him a seductive smile. "That would make it very interesting."

He looked back at her foot. Jimi drew in a soft breath as he carefully cleaned the cut, applied ointment and then a bandage before glancing at her. Jimi's heart fluttered when he smiled, tightening his fingers a little more on her foot.

"All done. You'll live."

Sensing the impending end to their intimate moment, Jimi decided it was time to make her move. She slid forward and, not breaking eye contact with him, reached out and curled her fingers around his neck. His muscles under her fingers were hard and his skin warm. As if her fingers fused to him and captured his energy, their connection crackled with electricity. He seemed to resist against the pressure of her hand. Jimi was insistent. When she pulled him toward her, she saw a myriad of emotions race across his face, and for a moment she thought he would pull away. But he didn't and gave her that crooked smile again. Her gaze dropped to his lips. His enticing and oh-so-kissable lips. Lips she wanted to taste, feel, explore.

When he dropped to his knees on the floor in front of her, Jimi gasped. He curled his fingers around her ankles and pulled her closer, holding her ankles behind him before letting go. Jimi hooked them together around his hips and shivered as he ran his hands over her calves, along her thighs, and grabbed her waist. Jimi wiggled to reduce the distance between them. The urgency to feel him next to her had her strung tighter than a drum.

"You're trembling," he whispered, and lowered his head so his mouth brushed tantalizingly close to her earlobe.

"I—I know." Jimi could barely form words, he had her so spun.

"I like that." His lips pressed in the curve of her neck.

"Oh, you're killing me."

She moaned as his lips tickled along her neck, his breath warming her skin until she thought she might melt right into him. He was everything male. His essence enveloped her and she craved more of him. A totally random thought flitted through her brain. *I'm made for him.* Then it was gone when his hands roamed over her, stealing all coherent thought. One hand went up to the back of her neck, under her hair to swipe it aside, the other down to her butt. She gasped as he pulled her tight, his fingers digging almost painfully into her flesh. But that pain brought such sweet pleasure she wanted more.

Jimi tightened her thighs around his hips, pressing into him, until her breasts were mashed against the unbelievably hard chest. He groaned and she thrilled to the sound. His fingers thrust into her hair, fisting the strands, and the sting in her scalp was another welcome burst of pain that almost kept her grounded.

He pulled her head back gently, forcing her to look at him. Jimi was at an utter loss for words. She wanted him, and he gave every indication he wanted her, the evidence of that pressing hotly between her thighs and only separated by the layer of their jeans. Jimi tipped her hips and sighed when he responded by thrusting into her.

"I can tell you're going to be all sorts of trouble," he growled.

"Is that a good or bad thing?" Jimi murmured, not breaking their gaze.

Her heart hammered so hard it hurt. This man—she still didn't know his name—held her hair tight while his other hand scorched a path from her ass up her side. He hesitated ever so briefly with a gentle caress at the side of her breast before cupping her face, holding her in his large, warm, rough…but so tender hands. She welcomed the control he was taking. Needed him to force her to let go. Her brain shut down when he pulled her head to him and crashed his lips over hers.

DALLAS TASTED HER as if a starved man. Her lips were soft and deliciously plump. He found her tongue with his, which was his undoing. Heat erupted inside him, flowing through his veins like thick, heavy lava. The sweetness of her mouth made him want more.

Her arms tightened around his neck. Dallas took her face between his hands, holding her firm. No way was he letting this seductress out of his arms just yet. Dallas opened his eyes to watch her, keeping his mouth fused with hers. The strands of her hair twined with his fingers, so *palupalu*, soft, he wanted to draw the curls over his face. He inhaled, taking in her scent. Fresh and clean, with a hint of flowers. Her eyes were closed, and he lifted his mouth from hers and waited to see if she'd open her eyes. She didn't, and he decided the eloquent curve of her brow needed to be kissed. Her gold lashes fanned across her pale skin. Never had he seen anything more beautiful. Sexy. And wanton.

Dallas nuzzled her under the sharp arch of her brow. She sighed. His cock swelled when she wiggled closer, tightening her thighs around him. He could easily push her back on his cot. Flick open the buttons of her shirt. Whisk off the jeans and take his pleasure. Pleasure she seemed very willing to provide.

Pleasure he'd be more than willing to reciprocate.

Jimi leaned into his fingers when he teased the buttons open. She trembled and he yearned for her. This strange and beguiling city girl who did not fit into the wilds out here. Or with a man like him. Perhaps that was what made her so much more tantalizing. Why not have a vacation fling? What happened in Kona stayed in Kona. No one need know. It would be over after the wedding. He'd keep it secret, knowing he was breaking his own rules.

A shiver rumbled through his muscles when her fingers tracked across his back, pressing and stroking as if she were trying to imprint him. Then they locked behind his neck and she burrowed against his chest. His hand was trapped between them in the wonderful firm softness of her breasts. Their clothes were in the way and he wanted to rip them off her in this frantic moment of passion. Period. Nothing remotely close to making love. Yet, if he thought of it as lust, an unsettled feeling grew in him.

Dallas pushed it aside. Being with a beautiful, alluring woman with no expectations or ties was just how to lose himself. There was no crime in that.

Jimi sighed as he nibbled the edge of her jaw. Dallas growled in to her and inhaled her wild and exotic scent that was just like his island. He'd learned long ago to seek out those special little places on a woman—it was so worth the extra care—and he found the delicate spot just behind her ear. Jimi's body went lax in his arms. She ran hands down his back, leaving a trail of heat that spiked into fire when she linked her thumbs through the belt loops and pulled him to her. He settled between her thighs, her heat searing him. Sound dimmed. All he heard was the thumping of his heart and her soft, breathy sighs. Jimi dropped her head back, giving him

more access, and he didn't waste the opportunity to
search for her trigger spot, smiling when she shivered
as he licked along her collarbone.

Voices pierced his lust haze. He tried to ignore them,
but when he recognized the laughter, Dallas swore
and sat bolt upright, pushing her away. Regret washed
through him at the confusion on Jimi's face and he
wanted to explain but couldn't. She stood and shoved
her hands into the jeans pockets.

She was mad—that was good. It made things easier.
He'd been ready to take it just a little too far with her.
Now wasn't the time or the place. He stepped back and
tried not to notice her passion-filled gaze, now tinged
with anger. Or the way her hair was mussed and the
plump pout of her mouth…all beckoning him like a
siren, calling him back to her.

"What…?" Her voice was soft and sultry, but he
heard anger around the edges.

"You'd better leave." Dallas did his best to keep
his voice unemotional, but he sounded like a bullfrog
croaking.

"What happened? I don't understand." Yep, she was
mad.

Before he could answer, a loud, booming voice from
outside the tent announced his brother.

"Dallas, you old dog, are you in there?"

Dallas stepped in front of Jimi to shield her while
she fumbled with her shirt buttons. The tent flap was
yanked aside and his brother filled the opening.

"Hey, bro! What the frig…" He gave a knowing nod,

raised his eyebrows and crossed his arms over his chest. "…ahh."

Jimi stepped around Dallas and he bit back a smile when he saw her lift her chin and shake her head, making her curls flutter around her shoulders like a lioness's mane. She flickered her gaze to Dallas, but he couldn't read the expression. It was as if a shutter had closed, hiding the light that had been shining from her only moments before. Strangely, it saddened him. He turned to Tucker and sent him a warning look.

"Excuse me." Jimi took a step and winced. Dallas reached for her elbow, but she shook him off.

"Don't let me interrupt things," Tucker said, his mouth curving up on one side.

"Yeah, yeah, enough of that. Tucker, this is one of our guests. She cut her foot on a stone and I was just doctoring her up."

"Yes." Jimi looked down at her foot. "It doesn't pay to not wear shoes around this godforsaken place. What a big mistake it was coming here." Without a second look, she pushed past both the men and sailed out the tent opening.

They watched her go and remained silent for a few seconds. Tucker turned to Dallas and burst out laughing.

"What the hell was that all about?"

Dallas thinned his lips and glared at his brother. Ever the loud one with no tact. "Nothing," Dallas snapped. The last thing he wanted to do was explain his actions to his brother. The less he knew the better, and no way would he let on what had almost happened.

"Well, bro, it certainly didn't look like nothing to me."

Dallas turned his back on him and grabbed the first-aid paraphernalia, holding it to Tucker as proof, then put it back where it belonged.

Dallas ushered Tucker to the tent opening. Time for him to leave. "Wasn't sure you'd actually show."

"You know me—I'm like a bad penny. Always turning up."

"You got that right. When you're needed, you're not here. When you're not needed, you turn up and usually with complications." Dallas followed Tucker from the tent. "So what brings you up here? Did you drive or ride?"

"Drove. I need to make myself scarce."

Anxiety squeezed Dallas's chest. "And you have to do that…why?" He'd had about enough of bailing his younger brother out of all the trouble he was good at getting himself into. Did he really want to know what he'd done this time?

"Oh, nothing. Just a little misunderstanding." Tucker drew in a sigh and stopped, turning to face Dallas. "Do you really want to know?"

Dallas narrowed his eyes and planted his feet, crossing his arms over his chest. He stared hard at his brother before answering. "Unless it's got something to do with jail, murder or losing the ranch, then no. Fair warning, though—don't make a fool of yourself or the family. I've—we've—worked too hard to keep our upstanding reputation. I don't need you to bring it down by doing anything stupid."

The look that flashed through Tucker's eyes wasn't what Dallas expected. He saw relief, pain in them and something else…defeat? Ah, shit, maybe he did need to know. He was his brother, after all. Under his cavalier and crusty exterior, Tucker was a softy. To the bone. Dallas had been hard on him, hoping the tough love would work. Last thing he wanted was his brother to fall down the rabbit hole again. "Like I said. Not unless it falls into any of those categories. But know that I'm here for you."

Tucker nodded and Dallas was relieved to see the stress ease a tiny bit from around Tucker's eyes. "I brought the truck. A few bags straggled in and Larson sent up some more wedding trinkets."

"More wedding crap? Take a look around—there's enough lace and ribbons and girlie stuff to sink a ship. What more could possibly be needed?"

Tucker shrugged a shoulder. "Who the hell knows. It's chick stuff. Anyway, we need to get it unloaded."

Dallas followed his brother to the half-ton dually. The wranglers had unloaded most of the additional supplies and late luggage, and carried stuff into the storage tent under Samantha's care. He checked the labels on the suitcases. Nothing for anyone named Jimi.

"Did Larson say anything about the other suitcase coming?"

Tucker shook his head. "She said something about a woman upset her bag hadn't arrived."

"Yeah, she's already made her displeasure known. Hopefully it turns up in the morning," Dallas muttered.

"So what's first now?" Tucker inquired.

"We should get the coals lit. Easy dinner tonight— everything's on the grill." He checked his watch and then looked to the sky. "Probably should get the guests out to Bridge Rock. The first night is supposed to be a sunset-cocktail thing."

"Seriously?" Tucker shook his head and gazed around the camp. "This really is a stretch for us, isn't it?"

Dallas nodded in agreement. "All I can say is thank God for Samantha. I didn't want any wedding responsibilities. This is important, though. If we can pull this off, it could open up a whole new niche for us. Weddings and glamping. I think there's a market."

Tucker gave him a skeptical look. "Where did you get that idea? I thought all brides wanted to be pampered, five-star, not roughing it like we are up here."

Dallas shook his head. "Apparently not, according to Sam. If there's a need, I will provide. Be warned and on your best behavior. Nothing is to go wrong. And no fraternizing, either."

"What, *moi*? Fraternize?" Tucker gave him a devilish look, but Dallas kept his demeanor stern. Tucker had to understand the importance of professionalism, something Dallas would have to remind himself where Jimi was concerned.

"So who is this wedding planner?" Tucker asked.

"Haven't you met Samantha Ray? She's Larson's friend."

Tucker shook his head. "Can't say that I have."

"They met at college, but she's not like Larson at all." Dallas looked over Tucker's shoulder. "Well, speak of the devil."

Tucker turned around as Samantha approached. She was a small thing. With red hair that hung in a riot of organized ringlets almost to her hips and pale blue eyes under ginger brows that easily drew you in, she exuded a serenity unlike Larson. Sam was calm, where Larson was wild.

"Well, well. No, I haven't met her," Tucker muttered in a low voice. "She might be worth a little bit of a chase."

Dallas found that funny and chuckled. "I think she'd run you a merry chase, that's for sure. She's way out of your league, bro."

Tucker ignored him, but Dallas saw the muscle in his jaw twitch, usually a sign he'd been offended. But sometimes the truth hurts and it needed to be heard.

"Hey, Sam, everything good?" Dallas asked.

"So far so good." She gave a bright smile and turned to Tucker, sticking her hand out. "Hi, I'm Samantha, wedding planner extraordinaire."

"Tucker, the evil brother of Larson and this *paniolo* here."

Dallas watched him take Sam's hand. They both fell silent and stared at each other for a little bit too long. Samantha's Tinker Bell mannerisms were momentarily quiet as she gazed up at Tucker. Dallas looked from one to the other. He sensed the attraction between them. They were polar opposites.

"Right, then. Anything else we can help with or do you just want us to disappear?" Dallas nudged Tucker out of the way, which forced him to drop Sam's hand. "Here, you take this last box, Tucker." He pushed the box with his boot until it was between him and Sam.

"Um, thanks." Sam's gaze lingered on Tucker as she bent to reach for the box.

"No, let me. I insist." Tucker reached and scooped it, hefting it into his arms. "Now, Miss Samantha, if you'll just show me the way…"

Her smile was bright as she spun on her heel and walked off, fingers sweeping her phone, red curls bouncing jauntily. But not without a little side glance and cute smile at Tucker.

Dallas sighed as he watched the two of them stride off. He wondered what sort of catastrophe was waiting to rear up next.

4

JIMI HAD NO WORDS. The sight held her spellbound, and she was stunned when tears pricked at the back of her eyes. A sunset had never moved her so deeply. She stood in hushed silence along with the rest of the wedding guests. All facing west watching the sun slip to the horizon.

She hadn't wanted to hike up to this ridge while they were told the barbecue was being readied, but, boy, was she glad she had. She'd been too ready to hang on to her misery, tucked away in her tent, but Jimi realized that was stupid. Rather than being a party pooper, she should join in. Make the best of a bad situation. A view like this was what she needed to remind her how good life truly was.

She hadn't been able to get Dallas out of her head and still felt his lips, the weight of his hand, his heat, keeping her at a slow burn of arousal. So, of course she looked for him. At least she knew his name now, thanks to his brother.

"Dallas," she whispered, letting the letters roll off

her tongue. She liked it. It was different and fit him so perfectly.

She glanced around—trying not to make it obvious—hoping to see him. She spied him off to the side leaning against a tree. It was like her gaze had found its home and she thrilled that he was watching her. Their gazes met and locked. The sunset momentarily forgotten. She didn't look away, didn't want to, couldn't. He gave her a leisurely smile, and her heart tumbled. She returned his smile, then turned back to the sunset, a new sense of excitement building inside her.

Brilliant hues of red and orange streaked the sky as the glowing orb set into the horizon. Wispy clouds reflecting in shades of pink chased across the sky above them. All too soon the sky purpled and darkened, giving way to the beginning of the velvet night.

No one seemed to move. Spellbound by the spectacle before her, Jimi wrapped her arms around herself and drew in a contented sigh. This really was beautiful.

"It's something." His deep voice was soft and low in her ear.

Jimi smiled and leaned back slightly, feeling his heat, almost like the air between them crackled with life. She nodded and breathed in the smell of the dusk air.

"It's quite a view. The way the land rolls down to the sea. I've never seen anything like it."

"So maybe being up here in the wilds of Hawaii isn't so bad after all?" She heard the humor in his voice and smiled.

Jimi turned to him and tipped her head back to gaze

into his eyes. "Maybe it's not. At first I thought being on this farm—"

"Ranch," Dallas corrected her gently.

She smiled. "Ranch, then. This isn't anything like where I grew up."

He looked down at her, and in that moment she knew they would be together. "Where did you grow up?"

She pressed her lips and wasn't sure what to say. She glanced at him and figured she'd never see him after the wedding right, so what did she have to lose? "Believe it or not, I grew up on a commune. Do you know anything about that lifestyle?"

"Only what I've read or seen on television."

"Trust me, it's not all it's cracked up to be. So I've tried to avoid any kind of farm or country life since." She rested her head back on his shoulder and looked up at him. There was something about him that called to her and she was eager to find out what that was.

"I've never met a woman, other than my sister, who enjoys country life."

"But this is beautiful." Jimi had begun to relax, even if she *still* didn't want to be here. "There's been nothing but surprises from the moment I stepped off the plane. You being one of them." Jimi rested back into him. "Everything is playing out so perfectly."

"That's the wedding planner's job. I only know the basic plans."

"Well, that's not really what I meant." Jimi didn't look away from him, not wanting to break the connection. She needed to see his eyes, those wonderful eyes, and maybe be able to see what was lurking in their depths.

His eyebrows rose. "Really?"

"Surely you have some idea." She smiled and her knees almost buckled when his lips curved up in return. But his eyes were shuttered. He was holding something back, even though his smile seemed to promise all sorts of tempting possibilities. There was depth to this man. She liked it and the challenge he posed. He held an air of authority, determination and compassion. A curious combination.

"Maybe some. Why, did you have something particular in mind?"

Jimi was enjoying their back-and-forth bantering. It was fun. Suggestive. And delightfully flirtatious. She was adapting quickly to her strained circumstances and hadn't thought of her lost suitcase in a while, mainly thanks to him.

"I might have something in mind." Jimi reached out and laid her palm on his hard chest. It seemed a completely natural thing to do, even if it was deliciously dangerous. His body heat warmed her palm and scorched up her arm, rushing through her blood, hot and heavy. She had a difficult time breathing as her desire settled with seductive heat deep inside her. Her nipples rose against the soft fabric of her borrowed shirt, which grazed the sensitive peaks. She trembled with anticipation.

Good Lord, there was *something* about this man.

Dallas drew in a sharp breath as if he felt the same electricity between them. His hand closed over hers and tightened momentarily before stepping away. "Perhaps we should explore the possibilities later."

Jimi nodded, drawing in a shaky breath, and took his cue, wandering off on her own. She glanced over her shoulder and watched him walk away, appreciating his magnificent male physique. Ranching had made him muscled, honed his body that clothing couldn't conceal. Jimi had the insatiable urge to rip off his clothes, desperate to see him naked. Her body temperature soared and it wasn't because of the Hawaiian heat.

"Hello! Everyone, please gather around." Jimi was glad of the distraction when the wedding planner called everyone. "The barbecue is about ready and the light is going fast. It's a tricky walk back down to our campsite, so how about we get a move on. And there are two special people waiting to say hi to y'all!"

Jimi smiled. That meant Diana and Matt had arrived. Then her heart dropped at the bad news she had to give her friend.

The wedding planner herded the group, but Jimi hung back behind a tree. She could follow them down and she ran a bunch of scenarios around in her head. She might be able to do something for Diana's wedding day. Oh, how she hoped her suitcase arrived tonight, or tomorrow morning at the latest. Rather than alarm Diana tonight, she'd hold off. Every bride's worst nightmare was her gown not showing up for the wedding. Jimi looked out across the waves to the darkening sky. It really was beautiful. Peaceful and serene. Something she hadn't felt in such a long time.

The voices faded. She was in no hurry to join them, rather liking the solitude. But she knew she shouldn't delay too long. Night was descending rapidly now that the sun was gone.

She turned around, and alarm flared inside her when she realized just how dark it was, making it difficult to see the path. She picked her way, trying not to trip over the loose stones, and listened carefully to hear the voices long down the path. Almost bumping into a tree, Jimi raised her hands and felt her way through the brush. While this was a beautiful country, she could see how quickly it could turn on you. Totally unprepared for this wilderness trip in Hawaii, Jimi swallowed the fear building inside her.

Being alone out here in the wild was a harsh reminder of her childhood. Getting lost in the bush and spending a night all by herself huddled and terrified in the root of a tree wasn't something you could easily forget. She kept moving one foot in front of the other—shuffling them over the ground—and stared into the darkness between the trees, hoping, waiting, for a flicker of light from the camp to show her the way. The icing on the cake would be for a storm to roll in. Jimi's heart clenched at the thought. After her mother died during a storm, she'd never gotten over her fear of them.

"Oh, thank God." Relief washed through her when she saw a sparkle of firelight off in the distance. The trail was steep and she had to take it to get down to the camp. Hopefully light from the torches would show her the way.

"I knew you were trouble the minute I laid eyes on you."

The deep, velvety voice in the dark made her jump out of her skin. "Oh! You scared the crap out of me."

She wasn't going to tell him how glad she was he'd come back for her.

"The last thing I need is for someone to get lost up here. Why didn't you follow the group down?"

She wasn't going to admit that she'd frightened herself. "I was so peaceful up there I wanted to stay a little longer. I was finding my way back with no trouble at all. There was no need for you to come looking for me."

"Right."

She heard the tinge of humor in his voice and knew he didn't believe her. That irked her. "So, lead the way, Tarzan."

"No need to get testy, Jane." He laughed, a low, slow chuckle that sent shivers along her skin. "You best take my hand—it's dark, and you can't see where you're going. I know how clumsy you are, too."

"I'm fine. Lead the way. And I'm not clumsy."

Jimi knew Dallas was standing in front of her by the darker form his body created in the shadows. He didn't move. Neither did she, until Jimi decided she wasn't going to wait for him to make the first move. They'd started something earlier, and she'd been yearning for it since. She had to get this man out of her system.

Jimi stepped into him, felt for his arms and grasped them. She stood on her toes and found his mouth with hers, sealing off any form of resistance. There was no fumbling, just his hot lips on hers.

Jimi sighed when his hands slid along her arms, took her wrists and lifted so she could wrap them around his neck. The musical night sounds and the warm, scented

Hawaiian air embraced them. Jimi lost herself in the moment.

Without the ability to see in the dark, all her other senses exploded into high alert. It seemed as if he touched her everywhere. The sultry tropical breeze whispered over her heated flesh, rousing her further. Threading his hands through her hair, he pulled her head back so she was at his mercy in the shadows. His lips, more powerful and insistent than before, had her melting into him. Her legs wobbled and Jimi clutched him tighter.

Night birds and other nocturnal animal sounds serenaded them as the creatures woke to their new day as the hour slipped deeper into the night. Leaves rustling in the breeze, distant voices from the camp, the tropical frogs and, mostly, their breathing was all she heard. Dallas's scent, warm, manly, was tinged with soap, leather and horse. He smelled so good she could eat him.

Jimi reached her tongue, wanting—no, needing—to find his. When the tips met, she moaned in ecstasy as molten fire flowed through her. He was magic, this man. This Hawaiian cowboy had the touch and she was thrilled to be at the receiving end of it.

He tightened his arms around her and shuffled her back until the solidity of a tree trunk pinned her sweetly between the rough bark and his powerful chest. Hooking a foot around his calf, she pulled so he had nowhere to go except closer to her. And like lava flowing over the craggy ground, he filled her. But not in the way she desperately needed. Jimi ached for him, and she clutched his shoulders, wanting him to take her here and now. In the dark. Under the rising tropical moon and rustle of leaves overhead.

"Now—"

"Easy, *hemahema*." His lips silenced her.

Jimi ran her hands up into his hair, and it fell over her fingers. Thick and soft, it made her want to discover more. He held her against the tree and she fell victim to his lips. Never had she been so thoroughly kissed. It was exquisite—the delicious fusion of their mouths, the way their arms held each other, the feelings that exploded inside her.

All from a kiss.

She moaned into him and he pressed deeper. His tongue danced with hers lightly, then firmly, only to tease her again. He was wooing her with his mouth, and she was falling for him in the most elemental way. His hard body pinned her, and she felt his erection nudge her belly.

Jimi felt like a schoolgirl again and she loved it. This man made her feel it was okay to let go—not hang on so tight—and give up her control, handing it over to him. She sensed it deep inside. He was safe. Hadn't he come to find her in the dark? After what seemed like a sweet eternity, he broke the kiss. His breathing was ragged, just like hers.

She was desperate to see his face, the expression in his eyes, but the dark hid him from her. "Take me to your tent. Or mine. I don't care."

"What I'll do is take you back down to the camp. The tent can come later when everyone is asleep."

He slid his hand from her neck, along her shoulder and down her arm, taking her hand in his. He left a charged trail of excited nerve endings where he touched her. Dallas tugged her and she followed him in the dark. "I'll hold you to that, cowboy."

He chuckled. "I had no doubt that you would."

Jimi smiled and her heart did a little tumble.

Dallas led her into the camp by the long barn, where she'd first fallen into his arms. The bright light from camp beyond the barn caught her attention. She was surprised at how much it had changed since the trek up to the ridge.

It was almost…pretty.

Through the trees and past the tents, she saw torches and twinkle lighting strung through the trees. Tables had been covered with some kind of cloth, and wide leaves with flowers grouped into them sat in the middle as centerpieces. The backs of chairs were draped with more flowers and leaves, as were some tree trunks. Torchlight lit the paths between the tents. It had a magical look, like a tropical fairyland, and Jimi loved it! Now she wanted to see what else had been done in the way of decoration.

"Just a quick walk through the barn to make sure the horses are all settled. That way, if we're spotted no one will think anything," Dallas told her as she followed him into the barn. The horses were dozing in their stalls.

"I don't really care if anyone thinks anything," Jimi confessed.

He stopped halfway down and turned toward her. "Well, I do. This is business, and reputation is very important to the family. I wouldn't want it to get around that a guest had been taken advantage of."

"I'm a big girl and can make my own decisions," she

retorted and immediately regretted her words, feeling contrite not considering it from his perspective.

"I bet you can." Dallas smiled. He had such an easy nature, and she was captivated all over again as he leaned down to her. "But I have to insist. Ranch rules and all that."

"Well, rules are made to be broken, yes?" He was going to kiss her again, and she waited, looking up at him with desire for this man that was unparalleled. She sighed with regret. "I understand. I wouldn't want to jeopardize your job. I still can't understand why she didn't choose a beach wedding! Isn't that what a destination wedding truly is? I don't think I'd consider a wedding like this."

Dallas didn't reply, and Jimi was surprised to see a strange expression cross his face. He stepped back, and she furrowed her brows when he turned away. Had she said something wrong?

"We best get back to the group."

"Um, okay." She was confused by his sudden mood swing.

"Looks like they've got the meal close to ready."

This time he didn't take her hand as he walked away. Jimi stood for a moment before following him. Why this sudden change of mood? Well, she wouldn't chase him down. No skin off her nose if he didn't want to hook up; while she was disappointed, she'd get over it and life would go on. But as she watched him go, all broad shoulders and slim hipped, Jimi made a decision that was the total reverse of what she'd just told herself. She wanted that man. And she was going to have him. One way or another, she'd be in his bed tonight.

5

JIMI FOLLOWED DALLAS into the twinkling light where all the wedding party guests had gathered. The fairy lights, flowers and decorations that totally screamed a wedding were a complete contrast to how all the guests were dressed. It rubbed Jimi's fashion sense the wrong way. Western wear, in Hawaii, and pretty sparkly wedding decorations shouldn't fit together, but they did. It was utterly perfect.

Glancing down at her own borrowed Western clothing, she realized she fit in dressed like this. Jimi didn't feel self-conscious at all. Lifting her hand, Jimi smoothed her hair, which had erupted into a wild riot of curls. She smiled. It would take some getting used to, not being perfectly turned out. But for now she allowed herself to feel comfortable and enjoyed the fact that she blended in.

She watched Dallas weave through the crowd, smiling at everyone and being the perfect ranch host. Jimi also saw the hungry look in the eyes of the women. Whether married or single, they lusted for him. A very unfamiliar feeling, something she hadn't felt since she was in the throes of puberty, turned her belly sour. She was jealous. It was hard to watch Dallas show the other women appropriate attention right after he'd kissed her senseless in the dark.

She shifted on her feet and pulled her gaze away from him. Jimi was determined he would be hers at least tonight for a little while. She could see no harm in a holiday fling. Her life back home was far too complicated to allow for any kind of relationship building. Especially a long-distance one.

The energy of the party took hold and she mingled, talking to people she didn't know. Then—surprise!—she spied a familiar face over by the bar.

She strode over and tapped the woman on the shoulder. She turned and a big smile lit her face.

"Holy shit, is it really you? Jimi!"

Jimi laughed and they fell into each other's arms. "Yes. It's so good to see you, Wendy."

"You too. Gosh, it's been years."

Jimi squeezed her and they stepped apart. "I know. What, six years since we graduated?"

"Ugh, has it really been that long? You're making me feel so old now."

"Sorry. But, yeah, time marches on."

"Truth. What a cool place for a wedding, don't you think? I was wondering how Diana would pull this off. So, how are you doing? Still designing?"

Jimi nodded and placed her hand on Wendy's arm. "Yes, oh, my God, you have no idea how excited I am. I'm designing Lilly Weaver's Oscars gown."

"The actress! Really? Holy shit, that's awesome! What's it look like?"

"You know I can't tell you that—it's a huge secret. The next few months will be ridiculously insane! But I so hope it is the beginning of more," Jimi said, polishing off the mai tai and reaching for another. "Jeez, these are good."

"Yeah, no kidding." A long, low sound startled them. Looking around, Wendy whispered, "Oh, look. A conch blower. There's Diana and Matt."

The wedding planner raised her hands, silencing the crowd. Funny how such a little thing of a woman held such commanding power.

"Good evening, ladies and gentlemen. I'm Samantha, your host and wedding planner for the next three nights here in beautiful Hawaii. The future bride and groom are in the house, so, please, let the festivities begin!"

Everyone clapped, hooted and whistled as Matt swept Diana back and kissed her. They looked so happy it made Jimi's heart hurt. Would she ever find love like that? They looked so damn happy. It made her wonder if she could ever have that one special relationship for herself. A man who would treasure her, be her true love and not take off when he got bored.

The crowd surrounded the couple and the smell of food wafted on the air, reminding her she hadn't eaten anything all day.

"I'm starved. Are you?" she asked Wendy.

Her friend shook her head. "No, I had a late bite after the never-friggin'-ending flight."

"Mind if I go over and get something?"

"Go, go. Of course not. Catch up with you later."

"Great." Jimi gave Wendy a hug and was surprised that her feet didn't really want to do as she bade them to. Must be those mai tais. She made her way to a beautiful table under a string of twinkling lights. She swore the table was groaning under the weight of food. Beelining to the stack of plates, she filled one and grabbed a glass of water. After finding a spot at a rustic table, she sat down, ate and watched the crowd.

The whole time watching for him, as well. He must've slipped away while she was talking to Wendy. It seemed that most of the ranch hands had disappeared. Her heart dropped with disappointment.

"Jimi!"

Jimi turned to see the bride-to-be approaching her with her arms wide. Standing, she greeted her. Ever expressive, Diana had her in a bear hug.

"Oh, Jimi, I'm so glad to see you and it's been way too long. Emails and phone calls just don't cut it."

"I know. I wouldn't miss this for the world. I'm very happy for you."

"So what you think?" Diana waved her hand around, indicating where they were. "Pretty cool, huh?"

"It's amazing. It really is." As she spoke the words, Jimi realized she truly meant it. "How on earth did you ever manage to make this look so fabulous?"

"It was Matt's idea. I thought a destination wedding should be on a beach, really. But when he suggested it, and after my initial resistance, I could see how wonderful it would be here. We are going to have a little bit of a party down at the Four Seasons next week. Plus, the wedding planner did the whole thing. She's a friend of the ranch owner's daughter, so..." She shrugged a slim shoulder.

"Oh, really?" That excited Jimi to no end, the party down at the Four Seasons. "That will be fun. I should have my suitcase by then."

"What do you mean? You don't have your suitcase? What happened to it?" Diana fired questions at her, which totally opened her up to the inevitable sharing of bad news.

Jimi shrugged her shoulders and held out her arms, trying to keep it light. "It got lost somewhere over the Pacific. They're hoping it'll arrive tonight and bring it up to me tomorrow. In the meantime... I have these wonderful clothes."

Diana leaned toward her and whispered, "Where did you get them? I'm so sorry this happened to you because I know how important having all your creature comforts is to you."

Jimi was sure she wasn't poking fun at her. Diana knew she was a fashionista. It was what she did for a living, so naturally it rolled over into her everyday life. But she wasn't that rigid or unable to survive without her clothes, makeup and shoes...or was she?

"It's fine. You have to make do, right?" She smiled and took a deep breath, ready to tell her about the wedding dress, surprised Diana hadn't asked about it.

"Where'd you get these clothes, then?"

"You have some very generous friends. I should be fine until my bag arrives. In the meantime I'll enjoy the rustic, new me."

"Oh, say, you have no idea how thrilled I was when you offered to design my wedding dress. It's not every day a girl gets a haute couture wedding dress."

"Oh, please, I'm far from haute couture. But…" Jimi waggled her finger at Diana. "You could have told me it was a country wedding and not a beach wedding." She also decided then and there not to say a thing until the last possible moment. Like the morning. If there was no suitcase by then, she would tell Diana and figure out what she could do for a gown for her friend.

"I know and I'm sorry. But whatever you have designed will be perfect. I just know it."

Jimi smiled and then found her gaze wandering off to scan the dancing guests.

It wasn't until Diana pointed it out that she realized what she was doing. "Who are you looking for?"

She'd been looking for Dallas. Yes, she'd been paying attention to Diana and at the same time unconsciously looking for the hot cowboy who had turned her inside out.

"Oh, just seeing if I know anyone here. I found Wendy a little while ago." She smiled at Diana, hooked her arm through her friend's and walked her over to the buffet. "Let's get a mai tai, even if I really shouldn't have another one, and catch up. Tell me about this man that has captivated your heart and whisked you off to the wilds of Hawaii."

"Let's! I'm dying to see my dress!"

"I'm dying to see you in the dress, too." *Oh crap. Here it comes.*

"Matt is wonderful—"

"Of course he is—you're marrying him." Jimi squeezed her friend's arm. She was truly happy for her and wanted to steer her off the dress course for now. God, how she prayed it would arrive. Not only for Diana, of course, but Jimi had committed to an interview with a top fashion magazine, and they were waiting for images to put in the photo spread. They were interviewing her because of her diversity. Oscars to destination wedding. Jimi groaned and looked up at the starlit sky. Anxiety gripped her belly. She tamped it down and looked at Diana, hoping it didn't show on her face.

"Yes, he is. It took a while for him to convince me, though. His patience paid off." She sighed, and Jimi felt the warmth of the feelings her friend had for her man. Clearly, he'd swept her off her feet.

"Diana!" A male voice boomed under the canopy of trees.

Diana spun around, a bright smile on her face. Jimi looked off in the same direction and watched a tall, redheaded man approach. He was sporting a smile that could brighten any gloomy day.

"It's him," Diana whispered, her eyes sparkling with excitement.

"Don't worry—I'm still allowed to see you before the wedding. I don't believe in bad luck and all that crap." Matt swept his bride-to-be into his arms and spun her around. Jimi watched as he placed her back on her feet and slid his hands down her arm to clasp her fingers in his.

Jimi was surprised at the flash of envy she felt.

"Attention, everyone." Matt raised his voice above

the din of the crowd, and momentarily everyone fell silent. "Aloha. And mahalo for coming all the way to wonderful Hawaii. I hope you're comfortable in your tents, and if you need anything just ask our fabulous wedding planner, Samantha. Please give her a round of applause for setting up this wonderful event."

He turned, indicating a woman who was standing beside a tree.

"Thank you, Matt. This is your day—I mean yours and Diana's. I'm a behind-the-scenes person charged with making your wedding spectacular. Thanks to Broken Creek Ranch for putting up with all my demands." She gave Diana a wink and continued, "Well, we may as well be clear. The demands were not mine, and all I can say is I'm thankful I don't have a bridezilla."

The crowd laughed.

"But, seriously, how could a wedding in Hawaii not be spectacular? I hope you enjoy yourself and, as Matt stated, please see me if you have any concerns or needs. I want to make your stay here as fabulous as the bride and groom's."

Samantha slipped away into the hush of the trees and all the guests began their chatter. Jimi took that as a cue to escape to her tent. A quick glance at Matt and Diana proved they wouldn't miss her. She was still hungry, though, and filled a plate to take back to her tent.

"I'm exhausted," she whispered to the darkness.

Juggling the plate and the mai tai, Jimi wove her way down the torch-lit pathways. A cozy couple approached her. They seemed totally in love, and as they passed, Jimi heard the man speak softly to the woman.

The man had an accent, and it was either South African or Australian.

"Hawaii seems to be our place, Lana. Who would have thought a wedding on a ranch could be as beautiful as one on a beach in Hawaii."

"I know, Grant. It's so lovely. Magical. I never would have thought it."

As they passed her, both looked up. "Evening," the man said, and the woman smiled at her. Jimi loved his accent.

"Good evening," Jimi answered, and returned the smile.

Yeah, they were totally into each other. It oozed off them and made Jimi feel lonely, while knowing deep down she would love that for herself. It wasn't on the horizon anytime soon, though. Maybe once she got her business more established, hopefully before she was old and gray.

Jimi sighed and found her tent. She stood in front of the open flap. The dark interior wasn't all that enticing. Despair rushed through her, as if going inside the tent would close the door on…something. She chewed her lip and glanced around. Mostly everyone was still partying under the twinkle lights.

A sudden gust of wind shook the tent and the trees overhead. Jimi inhaled the night air—seductive, warm, with the scent of rain, flowers and the tinge of leather and horses. Reminding her what Dallas smelled like. She wanted more of him and to finish what they'd started earlier.

DALLAS COULDN'T GET her off his mind. It was probably best for everyone involved, though, that he was in his tent alone and she was off doing whatever it was with the wedding guests and bridal party. He'd said it before and he'd say it again. She was trouble with a capital *T*. He felt weak around her. Look how he'd almost broken the ranch rules. He shook his head and tried not to think of her. It was impossible.

He wanted her. That, he couldn't deny. Being with her would go against almost every rule he'd ever set up for the ranch. Plus, it would only be a fling if it ever did happen. She was way too high maintenance and a complete fish out of water in this environment. A cowgirl she definitely was not. And if he was ever going to find a suitable partner, she would have to like, no—correct that—*love*, farm life. Being left at the altar wasn't something he ever wanted to experience again.

He swirled the Scotch in his glass before downing it in one gulp. The party was still hopping on the other side of the camp. Part of him wished he could be there having fun—*with her*. Dallas wondered if she'd found somebody to spend the night with. That made him grit his teeth, and a muscle jumped in his jaw. It was more proof that she was trouble for him if he was already feeling jealous over someone he barely knew. He reached out and was turning the lamp low, but his fingers froze when he heard a soft voice.

"Hello?"

Dallas turned to the tent opening. He hadn't dropped the flap yet. When he saw her standing there, his heart jumped and he surged to his feet. The chair skittering back to knock against the shelves.

"What are you doing here?" He didn't mean to sound

so harsh, but he was surprised as hell to see her. She
didn't answer and, instead, stepped inside the tent, turning around to drop the flap and tie it shut.

"I think we're adult enough to know the answer to
that."

Dallas watched her walk toward him. She moved with
a sensuality that had him breathless. Even in borrowed
clothing that was too big, baggy and hid her shape, she
fired every nerve ending in his body. She unbuttoned the
top until it hung open, exposing her flawless skin and
firm belly. He narrowed his eyes, then widened them
with delight when he saw a little flash on her belly. A
belly button ring. Dang! This filly might be a wild ride.

Slowly he raised his gaze, taking in everything, including the bra he'd seen earlier that held those tits he
longed to cup with his own hands. Everything in him
wanted to resist her, but there was something much
deeper that made him pause. He stared down into her
upturned eyes and saw something in them. Passion.
Excitement. Vulnerability. And something he couldn't
quite put his finger on but needed to find out. Screw
his rules. He'd rather be screwing her.

Dallas smiled and met her in the middle of the tent.
He liked the sound she made when he brushed his fingers over the jeweled piercing just above the waistband
of the jeans.

"You planning to lead me around with this thing?"

Jimi looked up at him and laughed, a deep, seductive sound that flowed under his skin, running like hot
lava about to erupt.

"Anything to hog-tie and get you into bed, cowboy."

"No beds here, or fancy ones, anyway. Just plain old cots."

She glanced at the cot and then back at him with a sexy grin. "I'm flexible."

"Now, that leaves room for interpretation, doesn't it?"

Dallas flipped the belly button jewelry one last time before sliding his hands over the warmth of her skin and pulled her to him. Perhaps a bit roughly, but she didn't seem to mind, coming quite willingly. Her arms wrapped tight around his neck and she pushed the back of his head down to her. He needed no encouragement, having already decided this was the path he was taking, regardless if it was a slippery slope. He stared into her eyes as he lowered his face to hers. Just before their lips met, her eyelids fluttered closed, and he did the same, losing himself in the feel of her. The taste of her lips on his and the sweet scent of her surrounded him.

He held her tight with one hand while his other one pushed the shirt off her shoulders. She lowered her arms and shook them a bit, encouraging the garment to slip down to the floor. Then her hands were on him, swiftly getting his shirt off him, as well. Dallas exhaled roughly, eager to see what was coming next.

They both reached for the front of each other's jeans at the same time and laughed.

"Seems we tend to think alike. But I wonder if you know what I'm thinking right now?" she purred.

"I never presume to know what a woman is thinking about at any given time."

"Smart man." She gave him a gentle push toward the cot. "How about we get this party started?"

6

HE WAS MAGNIFICENT. She couldn't get his clothes off quick enough. Desperate to feel his lips and hands on hers again, she reached for the front of his jeans. He was turned on—there was no doubt about that. After undoing the zipper, she cupped him, brazenly taking the first step. That was her undoing. Never had she been so aroused, excited about having sex. She wasn't about to ponder why—now wasn't the time. All she knew was she wanted them both naked, wrapped around each other.

He groaned, which spurred her on. Shoving down his pants, she quickly undid hers but couldn't get them off fast enough.

"Help me. This damn twine is in a knot."

Dallas kicked off his boots and stepped from his bunched-up jeans on the floor. He strode over to the cabinet where he'd gotten the bandages for her foot just a few hours ago. Jimi's mouth dried up at the sight of him. He was tanned, and his back muscles rippled as he moved and searched the shelves for whatever he was looking for. His tight black briefs emphasized his drop-dead sexy ass, and she was blown away by his muscular legs. She almost drooled as her gaze crawled over him, taking him in from top to bottom.

"This ought to do." His voice was thick with desire and made her belly do a little tumble. Jimi heard a click, and when he walked back to her with the blade in his hand she wasn't the least bit scared. She barely noticed he'd tossed something on the cot, as her attention was drawn to the front of his briefs. Jimi swallowed at the size of the bulge where his cock pressed. All she wanted was to whip off his briefs.

Her breath increased, and she was close to panting as he approached her with the knife in front of him. With a swift flick of his wrist, the baler twine she'd used as a belt fell away. No match for the sharp blade.

"Oh." She drew in a sharp gasp and her knees almost sagged. "That was rather erotic." She gripped his forearm, further reminded of how muscular he was.

She heard the knife clatter to the floor. Then his hands were on her hips, shoving down her jeans. A shiver rippled through her. She stood in front of him clad only in her bra and panties. But he'd seen that just a few hours ago, hadn't he? She gazed at him as he stood back and looked at her, openly scanning her body without any hint of propriety.

And she loved it.

"It's not fair."

"What's not fair?" His voice still so husky and deep it sent delicious shivers through her.

"You still have your clothes on."

He laughed and glanced down at himself. "You call this clothes?" He snapped the waistband of his briefs and stepped toward her, sliding his hands around her side and up her back until he cupped the base of her skull. "I call this pretty much even."

Jimi sighed as their bodies almost touched, a tease of what was to come as he pulled her closer. The thin space of air between them seemed electric. She laid her cheek on his chest, gently rubbing against the soft hairs curling across the broad expanse.

"Your hair seems to get curlier by the minute."

The pressure of his fingers on her skull was glorious. Even a gentle tug thrilled her. He pulled her head back until she looked up at him.

"I was cursed with kinky hair." She smiled, realizing the word she'd used.

"Is the girl as kinky as her hair?"

Before she could think of the right answer to his question, he shuffled her backward until the backs of her knees pressed against the wooden frame of the cot. Before she could blink, he had her sprawled on the quilts. This time she lay under his hot, heavy gaze. As he looked at her, Jimi found it hard to breathe. Her chest rose and fell as if gasping for air as she watched him stare at her. She couldn't take it any longer and reached for him. Grasping his boxers, she managed to get them down far enough that he sprang free.

"Oh, my." She swung her legs off the cot so she was sitting. Forgetting about Dallas's briefs, Jimi ran her palms up his powerful thighs to his hips. He groaned and thrust his fingers into her hair, drawing her closer to his erection. With one hand she gently cupped his balls while her other circled his thickness. Moving ever so slowly, she stroked him and was delighted as he grew even harder. She squeezed her thighs together, arousing herself even more.

"Keep that up and the show will be over before it had a chance to begin." Dallas removed her hands and put his finger under her chin, tipping her head up, and bent over her.

She gazed up at him with wonder. They seemed to go between frantic passion and gentle loving. She reached up and grasped his shoulders, tugging him down until his lips hovered over hers. "No more talk. Shouldn't we try and be quiet?" she murmured before silencing them both as she pressed her lips to his.

"I dare you to be."

"I can try."

Her body was craving more than he was giving. She wanted to feel his heat, the weight of him as he pressed her down. She thrust her tongue into his mouth and ran the tip of it across his teeth. That seemed to unleash the beast in him. The power and sexual being she'd been waiting for.

His hands were everywhere at once. Tangling in her hair, caressing her cheek, her neck. He unhooked her bra and pushed her back, never breaking the kiss. This was it—what she'd been longing for since she'd first laid eyes on this man. The soft quilts under her snuggled sweetly, a complete opposition to the rough and insistent man above her. His hand ran down her side and he hooked his fingers into the fabric of the panties at her hip. He pulled and they fell away.

He leaned back. Staring at her as if he touched her with his eyes. But her bra still clung to her, concealing her from his view. With what sounded like a frustrated growl, he reached for it and she knew he'd tear it off her. She didn't care. Briefly she thought of her lost luggage and this was her only set of undergarments, but all thought fled when he pulled the straps down her arms and tossed the lacy fabric aside.

He grabbed her hands and pulled them over her head, holding them with one hand while his other cradled at her neck.

"I knew you'd be gorgeous."

He gazed at her as if in awe. The hand at her neck slowly stroked down, across her shoulder until he cupped the side of her breast. She glanced down to where he touched her. His big and rough tanned hand, dark against her pale flesh, caressed her gently. She groaned and squirmed as her nipple rose. He sucked in a breath and brushed his thumb over the stiffened peak. Fire shot down to her pussy, but she couldn't tear her gaze away from the attention he was showing to her breast.

"So sweet." She barely heard his words and held her breath as his head lowered.

She inhaled a sharp breath when his lips sealed around her nipple, his tongue flicking and his teeth gently tugging on the tip. Like a live wire connected straight to her clitoris, Jimi bucked her hips. So close to losing control over herself. Her need for him beyond bearable.

Jimi clutched at his head, holding him tight to her

breast. So focused on the attention of his mouth, she was caught completely off guard when his fingers settled between her thighs. Insistent. Probing. Biting her lower lip to stop from crying out, she let her knees fall open. Dallas took the opportunity and moved between her thighs, cradling between them. Letting go of her nipple, he reared back and stared down at her. His eyes, stormy and passionate. He was the most wildly handsome man she'd ever known.

A flash of sadness surprised her.

Why? Because he was a one of a kind. A decadent distraction while in Hawaii, at her friend's wedding. Where a fling was just that—a fling—with no commitments for tomorrow. She had a life to go back to. A glaring opposite to his life.

Live in the moment. Forget about tomorrow. "Good idea," she whispered, acknowledging her mantra.

"Mmm, what are you mumbling about?" He smiled down at her.

"Nothing important."

He reached for something beside her head.

"Now, it's not gentlemanly to keep a lady waiting. Oh! I don't have protection with me." This couldn't be happening! Not now, not when she was craving him in such a powerful way.

"A gentleman always comes prepared." He held up the little foil package between his fingers with a very smug grin on his face.

"Who's the lucky girl! But you're still keeping me waiting."

Anxiously, she watched him rip open the package

and slide it down his cock. The way he moved his hands on himself had her breathless. She ached to feel him inside her. He hooked his hands behind her knees and pulled her down until her bum was resting on his thighs, her legs spread wide so she was fully exposed to his heated gaze.

Jimi trembled. Never had she felt so wanton, bare to the man's gaze before. She tightened her legs, feeling the need to close them.

"Relax, *hemahema*." A delightful shiver ran through her at the unique term of endearment. She rested back, her arms flung wide, fingers curling into the quilt.

She jumped when his hands rested at the crease of her thighs. His thumbs stroking so teasingly close to her center.

"Oh, you're killing me," she whispered. Squeezing her eyes shut, she focused all her attention between her legs. His touch went from soft and tentative to demanding. It was exquisite as he mapped her out. Pressing, seeking, sweeping his fingers through her folds. When he pushed into her while at the same time pressing on her clit, she moaned and rose to meet him.

"I want to see you come. Before I fuck you."

His fingers increased in pace. In and out, then curling against that most sensitive spot just inside her. The spot she thought was elusive and just a fairy tale. Oh, but this charming Hawaiian prince had found it. Coupled with his attention on her clitoris, and the way he knew how to stroke her, Jimi was lost. She was a raging bundle of desire, but she reached for him, needing and wanting to touch him.

"Don't. Just enjoy. Be in the moment." She heard the strain in his voice. It told her everything she needed to know. He was giving her this gift of selflessness. Making sure she was being fulfilled. Her heart filled and she focused on his voice. The unintelligible murmur of words. The deep, rumbly tone that swept her away.

His voice surrounded her like hot honey, as if giving her permission to not worry about him right now. So she let herself go. The dark behind her closed eyelids drew her down. She felt overwhelmed by him, and when that wonderful feeling rose in her belly she was lost. His fingers teased, touched, stroked and then rose to a demand that was almost fierce. Jimi held her breath, starved for oxygen, but no way could she draw in air. If she did, she would lose it. Lose the sensation. The rush of excruciating heaven that bore down on her.

Then, when she couldn't stand it any longer, her back arched and she let out a cry. That was immediately shushed by his lips on hers. She screamed into him as her orgasm rolled over her. She was boneless under him and he took her breath, drawing it in before giving it back to her once she had quieted. Jimi drew in a trembling sigh when his mouth lifted from hers. Slowly she opened her eyes to find his face hovering over hers.

"Th-that was—"

"Just the beginning."

Jimi felt like she could purr. She circled her arms around his neck and hooked her heels behind his butt.

"I'm so glad to hear that."

He reached between them. Seconds later his cock was at her opening. Still sensitive after her climax, when he pushed into her, she locked him to her. His head dropped and his hair fluttered over her face. Languidly, he pressed into her. He was taking it slow. Too slow.

"Fuck me. Don't be the gentleman you said you were. Not right now," she told him. "I want to feel you fill me. Hard and fast."

As if a different man were now above her, she felt his muscles tense. And he drove into her. Hard. She caught her breath when he filled her. She took him and matched him thrust for thrust, their cadence so powerful the cot jumped on the wooden floor. He reached his hand between them, and, finding her sensitive nub, he stroked in time with his plunges. She unleashed him even further. Gone was the softness he'd shown her, and in its place a roughness that she welcomed.

They weren't making love. They were using each other to each find their release. His breath was harsh, and she made a grunting sound as she clung to him. The rawness of their coupling was so different from the previous playful tenderness. Jimi wasn't able to put much thought into this as he swiftly carried her to another orgasm. It turned her inside out and, in that moment, her world tipped off its axis. She loved it. Loved that he was doing this to her. *With* her.

Jimi clutched at him, not wanting to let him go. How could she let him go? But he was just a fling. They weren't a couple. Just a man and a woman taking and giving pleasure to each other. Strangers that had crashed into each other's lives, making new tracks together. Tracks that overlapped. Tracks that she didn't want to ever think might part at a fork in the road.

She knew nothing would ever be the same again, but had no time to give it more thought when another orgasm crashed through her. She bit her lip to keep from crying out. He groaned into her neck, and she jumped when she felt his teeth nip her shoulder. This time he didn't kiss her to help silence her delight. The urge to pull away, slightly frightened by this new ferocity he was exhibiting, overcame her. But he still had her in the throes of coming. Coming hard, not once, but as his pace picked up and she sensed he was close, she rolled into another wild orgasm under him.

He tensed, pushed hard and deep into her. Growling like a bear as he came. Jimi clutched at his back, digging her nails in. She tipped her hips and tightened her legs around him, wanting him to have the same powerful climax he'd given her. He ground into her and she accepted him, until he went slack and, after a few moments, rolled off. He kept her in his embrace and Jimi didn't move. His heart pounded next to her cheek in time with how hers was beating. Tentatively she draped her arm across his belly. Dallas tightened his arm around her shoulder in a possessive grip that made her smile.

She couldn't think. Her brain was mush after the wild sex she'd just experienced with this dark and mysterious Hawaiian cowboy. As she lay there in the afterglow, his fingers lazily swirling circles on her shoulder, Jimi sighed. Happy. Content. Calm. Regardless of his intensity and almost frightening nature, not to mention her determination this would be a one-night stand only, Jimi knew she was hooked.

7

JIMI PULLED THE COVERS over her head and let out a screech at the crash of thunder that exploded right above her, jolting her from sleep. Her childhood terror of storms had never truly been resolved. She squeezed her eyes shut and waited for the next boom, absolutely frozen with fear.

It was louder than the first, and then a howling like a freight train roared down on her. Unable to emerge from the covers, she lay there terrified. *Where am I?* Too afraid to peek out from under the covers, Jimi forced her brain to clear the cobwebs. It dawned on her where she was as another earsplitting crash of thunder sounded like the Second Coming. Regaining her sense of place, she knew she was in the bed she'd just had sex and slept in with Dallas. She walked her fingers over the cold sheets. He was gone.

A flash so bright that it pierced through the layers of blankets and her closed eyes was followed by a deafening explosion. Jimi cried and curled into a ball, terrified by the seemingly end of the world going on outside around her.

Move, she screamed at herself. This was no normal storm that had come calling. It was different. *What if it's a hurricane and not just a violent storm?* Fear slipped its icy fingers down her spine and she let out a sob into the blankets. With everything that had gone wrong so far on this vacation, a hurricane would be the icing on the proverbial cake.

"Jimi!" The male voice on the other side of the blanket frightened her even further. It was the tone in the voice that had the hairs on the back of her neck stand up.

The covers were whipped off her.

"Get up and get dressed. Now. There's no time to lose."

"What's happening?" she asked as she bolted from the bed and quickly drew on the clothes that lay scattered over the floor. It was dark out and hard to see but the snapping sound of the fabric as the wind clawed at the tent was terrifying. "Is this a bad storm?"

"It could be. We're going to try and get back down to the main house."

"How's everybody going to fit in the truck? What about the horses?"

"We'll have to make do with what we have. And don't worry about the horses—a few of the wranglers will stay back. Now, hurry up."

Stepping out into the maelstrom was horrifying for her. Running under the trees that were bending to the demanding winds, and with lightning flashing overhead, she nearly froze.

"Come on. What's wrong with you?" Dallas reached for her hand and the warm strength sent a calming rush through her body.

"Not a fan of storms much." She tried to keep her voice from betraying her actual terror.

The rain was almost going horizontal and stung like needles.

A crowd of people had gathered beside the three vehicles—two open pickup trucks and one cube van. Dallas let go of her hand as he began giving instructions. She wondered what his role actually was here. The way he took charge and the way people listened to him suggested he was the lead ranch hand. She watched him through the slashing rain, and a sense of pride filled her as he responded so capably to this crisis and kept everybody calm.

Dallas shouted above the storm. "We should all fit. It will be tight, but there's no choice. We have to try and get down before the river blows its banks. So split up and climb in wherever there's room."

"What about all our stuff?" a voice asked before being drowned out by thunder that made Jimi shrink lower.

"No choice but to come back later. Time is of the essence. Get in the vehicles now."

He glanced reassuringly in her direction, and she smiled just as a tremendous crash of thunder ripped the sky open above them. She cringed under the sound and her knees buckled under her. It was useless, no matter how hard she tried. Overcoming her fear of storms wasn't going to happen anytime soon. She gripped the side of the pickup truck and pulled herself back to her feet.

A strong arm curled around her waist. She knew it was Dallas and relief flooded through her. Although she didn't want to be a burden to him under the present circumstances, she was glad he had come to her.

"You're coming with me."

He scooped her up and tossed her inside the truck cab, pushing her to the center and climbing up behind her. "Unlock the door. We can get more people in."

She did as she was told. "Get in," she told the couple waiting by the truck. They piled in, and it was tight with her, Dallas and two others sharing the seat.

"Is it safe to drive?" the woman beside her asked.

"If we get down before the river overflows the banks," Dallas answered, and put the truck in Drive.

Jimi sucked in a breath and turned to Dallas, her fingers curled into his thigh beside her leg. "What does it mean if that happens?"

She watched his jaw muscle twitch and knew she wouldn't like his answer.

"Then we're stuck up here until the water goes back down." He stepped on the gas and the truck lurched ahead, skidding on the now muddy road. He glanced in the rear-view mirror, then grabbed a walkie-talkie from the dash and spoke into it. "Get this convoy moving, folks. No time like the present. Follow me." He gave it to Jimi. "Hold this." She clutched it tightly.

"Holy shit." The woman beside her was beginning to panic. It started to rub off on Jimi's already rattled nerves. "This is horrible. I can't stay out here in the storm."

"Shh, just relax and everything will be fine," the woman's husband assured her.

Jimi leaned to Dallas and whispered, "Is this bad? Is it a hurricane?"

He glanced down at her briefly and gave her a reassuring smile. "It's a strong storm that came in fast."

"But will we be okay?"

"Yes, we'll be fine. Just uncomfortable until it passes."

"Then why do you seem so panicked? I hope we can pass the river and get back down. I don't like being up here like this." She heard her voice hitch and tried to hide it by clutching his arm and leaning into his comforting strength.

"I'm not panicked. I'm trying to get everyone down to the main house in one piece." He glanced at her. "You're afraid of storms."

She nodded, unable to voice such a stupid fear.

He kept his hands on the steering wheel, but she wished he was able to put his arm around her; instead, she had to calm herself by simply leaning into him. The truck bounced and skidded on the rain-soaked back road, succeeding in ramping up her alarm. Every manner of bad endings for the group trying to flee ran through her mind. What a wedding trip! She felt sad for Diana and Matt. A hurricane was a complete wedding crasher.

"Please, please just let us get out of here in one piece," Jimi whispered, and was pretty sure no one would hear her from the roar of the engine and storm around them. Her heart was in her throat and she buried her face into Dallas's arm. She did not want to know what was going on outside of the truck.

"Shit!" he shouted, and the truck skidded to a stop with such force both she and the two passengers beside her wound up on the floor in a heap. Dallas helped her and the other two scrambled back into the seat. "Sorry about that, folks."

He glanced into the rearview mirror as Jimi turned around. "Thank God, they didn't hit us."

"Exactly, or we'd be riding the river in this truck."

"What?" The lady next to Jimi cried out.

Dallas took the walkie-talkie from Jimi's clutched fingers. "Tucker, we need to back these trucks up. *Now, now, now!* The bridge is out. Back to the camp double time. Make sure everyone goes to the barn. And close those shutters."

The radio crackled. "Gotcha, bro."

Dallas turned in the seat, resting his arm across the back of it, and steered like a pro in the opposite direction. They bumped backward the way they had just come until he yanked on the steering wheel, finally able to turn around and get back to the camp. Jimi was breathless and in complete awe of him. He was so self-assured. In control. A new emotion took root inside her.

Dallas was out of the truck before anyone else. He reached in for her, stood her next to the truck and jogged into the crowd. Everyone piled out and huddled together waiting for instruction.

"Folks," Dallas shouted, and pointed at Tucker. "Follow him to the barn. Fast. It's the safest place right now until the rain lets up." Tucker turned and disappeared into the rain with a crowd following him.

Wiping the water from her eyes, Jimi hesitated and looked for Dallas. He was helping stragglers from the truck bed.

"Jimi," he shouted, pointing at Tucker, "follow him. I'll be there shortly."

She stood for a moment, the rain and wind slashing her face. She was soaked, miserable, terrified and cold. Yet she'd never felt more exhilarated. Maybe it was because of Dallas. The way he'd taken charge and kept everyone safe. Making her feel safe. A man you could depend on. She looked at him through the rain with new eyes. He was a complicated man. Depth, passion, compassion—she had to know more about him.

It was hard to leave him and do as he instructed, but she did and ran to follow Tucker.

As IF THINGS could be any worse. Dallas cursed the weather. He'd known something was bearing down, but he couldn't believe how fast the storm had grown into a monster and made landfall. Not only did he have guests marooned up here with an impassable road, they had to all hole up in the barn. Nice and cozy like and very uncomfortable. No beds, wet, and hot food to a minimum.

He sighed and ran through the sheeting rain to his tent. The canvas was close to shredded, thanks to the wind. The cot where he'd spent the night with Jimi was upturned against the side of the tent—he didn't bother righting it. So much for their cozy love nest. Any further hanky-panky with her would definitely be out now. And likely that was a very good thing. It would help him stick to the rules he had done a great job of breaking. Even if the thought of having sex with her made him want to break every rule in the playbook.

Sliding on the slick floor to the cabinet, he grabbed the portable first-aid kit, extra batteries and shoved them next to the walkie-talkie in his jeans pocket. Glancing around, he tried to decide what else they'd need for however long it took to ride out the storm.

The wind howled, shredding the canvas even more. It snapped like a bullwhip. The hell with anything else. They'd have to make do. He needed to get to shelter. Thankfully, the horseshoe ridge gave some protection from the wind; it was why he'd chosen this location for these camping expeditions. Struggling through the storm, he was glad to see the shutters had been lowered on the barn. Dallas squeezed through the narrow opening at the end and drew in a deep breath.

"Jessica!" He shouted for one of the wranglers. "I need you here." She ran over and he handed her the first-aid kit. "Take this and check that every one of the guests is fine. You've had first-aid training, right? Studying to be a nurse?"

She nodded.

"There should be paper in the feed room. Make a list of all the people, if they have any injuries and keep an eye on them during the storm. Off you go." Dallas looked around. The horses were jittery, but the hay kept them content. Too bad the wedding guests couldn't be placated as easily. They were lined up in the center aisle. Battery lanterns hung from the center rafter, giving the barn a cozy ambience despite the circumstances.

He searched for Jimi to make sure she was safely in the barn. He let out a breath when he saw her sitting with her knees drawn up, arms wrapped around them, her face buried and hidden by her hair.

Tucker was beside Dallas. "What a mess."

"You can say that again," Dallas agreed.

"You were right to reinforce the barn like this. Even though you got pushback about it. I can see now it was the right thing to do. Even if the odds of a storm like this are long." Tucker looked up at the roof, nodding.

Dallas nodded in agreement. "All tight?"

"Yep, we're good. But it's this lot that has to ride it out without everyone going nuts." Tucker cocked his head in the direction of the miserable-looking guests.

"What's Sam planning?" Dallas asked his brother.

"I couldn't tell you, bro. After the first introduction, I haven't had the chance to talk to her."

Dallas scanned the crowd. "There she is, with that group at the end of the aisle. Now might be a good time to offer up some help. Get in her good books right off the hop."

Tucker gave him a punch on the shoulder before making his way down to Sam. Dallas furrowed his brows and looked for Larson. His sister hadn't ridden up with them, and he wasn't totally sure she was even up here. Another sign he'd been far too distracted by Jimi to not even know where his own sister was. But he needed to find out, fast.

He shouted after his brother, "Tucker! Where's Larson?"

"At the house—she didn't come up."

Relief flooded through Dallas. Okay, now that he

had everyone accounted for, it was time to ride this puppy out.

He inspected every shutter, making sure they were firmly attached and that the horses were just as securely tied. He was glad he'd had the barn built with this sort of situation in mind. It wouldn't be glamping and they'd definitely be roughing it, but they'd make do. The cube van was backed up at the far end for access to supplies.

So much for all the paraphernalia he'd hauled up here for the wedding. But, all that aside, he had to find Diana and Matt. It was their wedding trip and their decision on how to proceed. Then he remembered the minister was to be driven up tomorrow in time for the wedding. Dallas checked his watch—three o'clock in the morning.

That wasn't happening anytime soon. He swore under his breath and tried his damnedest not to let his frustration show. This wedding event had been their foray into destination weddings. He'd been against it at first, thinking it was far too much risk for the ranch and its reputation, but Larson had been relentless. Pestering him until he'd agreed. She was right, though. Trying to grab wedding business from the big beach hotels was a good idea—but it had to go without a hitch.

He listened to the wind howl around the roof. "Shit." Dallas clenched his jaw and decided to make the best of the situation. If he could get everyone through this unscathed, then they might still stand a chance at positive reviews.

UNLESS SHE WANTED to cringe helplessly while the storm crashed around her, Jimi decided she had to take the bull by the horns and do something. Lifting her head, she pushed hair out of her face and wiped her eyes.

She scanned the dimly lit barn for Diana and Matt. How were they coping? Jimi pushed herself to her feet, determined to make every effort to overcome her terror and try to be of use to someone. Anyone. Thunder crashed, and she nearly crumpled back to the ground in a heap.

"Hey, there. It's not that bad, you know. We'll be fine." Dallas's deep voice was a welcome balm amid the maelstrom around them.

"Will we? It sounds really bad out there."

"Well, it isn't good, but I've been in worse." Dallas wrapped his arm around her shoulder and pulled her tight.

Instantly she felt safe and breathed out a ragged sigh.

"Being afraid of storms can be overcome," he assured her.

She looked at him, grateful for his attempt at calming her. "Yeah, well, I'm not so sure about that. I've tried more times than I can count, with no luck."

"What happened to make you so afraid?"

She didn't really want to dredge it all up, but the need for him to understand suddenly seemed very important. The last thing she wanted was for him to think her weak or silly.

"A bad storm when I was a child." She looked up at him and took a deep, quavering breath. "Um, my m-mom died." Not wanting him to say anything as she felt the edge of panic looming, and talking about how her mom died would be her undoing. "Maybe if I keep busy. What is happening about the wedding?"

"I'm sorry, Jimi. That's horrible." He hesitated and then asked softly, "Do you want to talk about it?"

She looked up at him but, while she appreciated his concern, she still couldn't find the nerve to verbalize how horrific it had been. "Not right now—it's too close to this." She waved her hand to the roof of the barn and the storm that raged outside. She switched the conversation to a safer topic. "Is there much we can do for the wedding?"

"NO. WE JUST have to ride this out." He took her by the shoulders and turned her. "It will be all right. This is a safe place. And I'm here if you feel overwhelmed or frightened."

She looked up at him in wonder. He was caring and concerned and a protector. All the things she yearned for in a man. "Thanks. I'll remember that."

A crash boomed and she cowered. Jimi had to think of something else, so she thought about Diana. She must be devastated. This also meant she wouldn't need her wedding gown right away. Jimi was glad she didn't have to dump the bad news on Diana about the dress, even if missing a wedding was way worse. A bride could only take so much.

"I think I'll find Diana and see what I can do."

"That's a great idea."

Dallas gave her a gentle squeeze. Jimi didn't want to leave the comfort of his arms, but she forced herself to.

"They're down at the other end of the barn." He pointed and Jimi looked in the direction he indicated.

"Okay. Well." She gave him a smile, which he returned, and then wove her way through the people crouched on the barn floor. As the storm surrounded them, almost shaking the rafters of the barn, she noticed the other guests had found ways to distract themselves and kill time. Their mannerisms comforted her, as well. So by the time she got to Diana, Jimi was almost feeling like her old self.

"Jimi! How are you holding up?" Diana asked. Jimi was surprised. For a bride whose wedding was being decimated, she looked like she didn't have a care in the world.

"I'm fine, but what about you? What a horrible thing to happen. It's completely set things back for you."

"Ah, we'll make do. You know what they say...rain on a wedding day is good luck."

"And this definitely looks like it's going to hang on until your wedding day."

Diana glanced toward the closed shutters and frowned before smiling brightly again. "It sure does."

"Aw, Diana, I'm so sorry." Jimi wrapped her arms around her friend and hugged her tight. "Listen, is there anything I can do to make it better?"

Diana hugged her back. A boom of thunder overhead made them both jump as they stepped apart. "No, nothing. You just try and enjoy yourself. I know it's a disaster. But it will all work out in the end. We're going to make it up to everyone at the hotel later. We do have to get married you know!" She laughed.

Jimi had to hand it to Diana. Under the circumstances, she sure was taking this all in stride. If it was her wedding? Well, Jimi had no idea how she would be handling things, other than likely not near as well as Diana was.

"Hey, honey, how you doing?" Matt came up and put his arm around his fiancée's shoulder, holding her tightly. Diana leaned into him and wrapped her arms around his waist as he dropped a kiss on her head.

"It's all good. We have no control over Mother Nature." She grinned at Matt, and Jimi knew she was putting on the brave front. "We'll be husband and wife soon."

"I've waited this long for you—a couple of days more won't hurt." Matt smiled at Diana, and Jimi's heart swelled. The love he had for Diana was evident and Jimi was happy for her. Jimi glanced around the barn. Her gaze fell on Dallas at the far end, and she watched as he moved around, checking the shutters, stopping to talk to guests, giving the horses strokes as he walked past them. She smiled when she noticed how each horse lifted their nose to him, almost as if they knew he would stop and give them a little bit of attention as he moved around the barn. Her heart told her he was a good man. And her body told her how much it wanted him.

From remembering the couple who had walked past her last evening at the barbecue, the romance and love oozing off them, to witnessing now the love between Diana and Matt made Jimi want that, too. How could she ever get a chance at love and a long-lasting relationship when she was so focused on her career, her business? Her independence?

Never taking her gaze from Dallas, Jimi felt both excitement and sadness. He was special, and it seemed impossible how quickly she'd grown attached to him in this short space of time. It was the intensity of the situation. Would they get a chance to see where it could go after all this?

Dallas stopped in the center of the barn. "People, attention for a moment."

Everyone stopped and turned to him.

"A bit of housekeeping. We won't be at a loss for food or water, so no concern there. We have a truck backed up to the barn at the far end for supplies. Now, as for facilities, you'll notice a cordoned-off area also at the far end. Sorry to do it to y'all, but it's back to the basics and rustic living. The shitter, as we call it, is in business."

He smiled a wide smile, and Jimi heard a few people, including herself, laugh.

8

"Is it safe to venture out?" Although Jimi had spent two nights and a day trapped in the barn, she was still a little nervous about leaving its safety, even if the rain did stop this morning. It remained dreary outside and she worried the storm would come back.

"Trust me. I know this land like the back of my hand." Dallas helped her on the horse. "The worst of the storm is past, and this will be a perfect time to show you."

"Will we head back down now that the storm is over?"

"Can't until the river lowers. So we may as well make the most of our time…and what better way than with a ride. Since you didn't get to ride up here in your fancy dress and shoes."

Taking the truck had been the wisest thing without proper riding clothes. Now that she had some borrowed ones, she was actually glad of going for a ride. When she thought back to just two days ago and how upset she was to be up here in the wilds, then the storm, this ride would be a welcome interlude.

"What about all the guests? We can't just take off and leave them."

"They'll be fine. Tucker, Samantha and the wranglers have them in hand. Plus, they've been good sports about this. Now that the weather is clearing up, they seem happy until we can head back down to the house."

"When do you think that will be?"

"Hopefully, by the end of the day. I'm sure everyone would be much happier back down in civilization. Including you." He grinned at her, then checked his cinch and gathered the reins, about to mount his horse.

For some reason his comment stung her. Did she really give off the aura of a diva, unable to enjoy life without all the finer things? She thought she'd done pretty well since the storm blew in. Being thrown back into rustic living had been a shock, something she hadn't wanted at all, and yet maybe this whole trip up here was a blessing in disguise.

A hard lesson to be sure, but making her see things in a different light.

Without her conveniences and not having to worry about looking perfect all the time was actually liberating. She hadn't realized until just this moment how caught up in appearances she was. And the cool thing was that Dallas didn't seem to mind her borrowed clothes, lack of makeup and riot of hair. He was seeing her at her worst and there was no judgment. He accepted her. In fact, if she thought back to the beginning, he'd never seen her perfectly turned out, which was her norm. Still, she wasn't ready to completely let go of her armor of clothes and makeup. She'd built that shell over years, and it would take more than a few days to break it.

Jimi watched him swing with ease onto his horse. Her heart beat a little quicker. He settled into the saddle and gathered up the reins. Jimi watched his hands, how he cradled the leather between his fingers. The gentle yet firm touch he had and the horse's response to him only reminded her how wonderful his touch was.

Oh, yes, there sure was something about him and not just physically—that was a given. There was more. His quiet, calm way. His strength. How he'd easily calmed her in the storm, constantly keeping tabs on her to make sure she was okay while also tending to all the guests. How he made her feel special. Like now, how he'd helped her on the horse—even though she was quite capable— checking the stirrups were right and placing her foot just so in them. The lingering touch of his hand on her knee. Everything about him was perfect. Jimi rested her palm where his hand had just been, positive she still felt his energy.

What was happening here? He was supposed to be just a holiday fling.

Glancing back at him, she smiled when his horse did a little dance. He was an excellent rider and looked so good in the saddle. She'd seen some men ride, men who should never ever have sat in a saddle. In fact, it had turned her off one or two. So, watching Dallas ride was sweet, indeed.

"Easy there, Sweeny." Dallas crooned to the horse, and the mare instantly calmed, falling into a nice ground-covering trot.

Jimi nudged her horse and followed suit. Used to riding English, she started to post, but her horse had a wonderful smooth trot and she was able to sit to with no problem.

"Hey, you look mighty fine in the saddle." Dallas gave her an appreciative smile.

"I've been riding since I was little, although not much in recent years. English, but I'm adaptable." She bit her lip and then started to tell him something she'd never told anyone before. "I rode on the commune. Of course, ponies to start, bareback with a halter. Then graduated to the horses."

"That doesn't sound too bad."

"That part wasn't." She drew in a breath and continued, "It was a hippie commune. Sure, there was free love, and all that, but not a very nurturing environment for the kids. We were left to fend for ourselves, like we were a by-product of communal sex. The only nurturing person was my mom. All the kids loved her." Tears pricked her eyes at losing her mom far too soon. "But anyway, like I said, I'm adaptable." And before she spilled any further private thoughts, she proved her point by giving the appropriate leg commands and the horse broke into an easy lope. She passed Dallas on the trail, with no idea which way to go.

"And by the way, what is it you want to show me?" she called over her shoulder.

His horse's hooves thumped on the trail, and in a flash he was past her.

"You'll see when we get there. That is, if you can keep up."

Jimi laughed and leaned over her horse's neck. Never one to back down from a challenge. Oh, she'd keep up, no doubt about that. They raced down the trail. Mud flew and the misty air soaked her in minutes. She was used to being wet after these last couple of days. Inhaling, she drew in a deep breath of the warm, tropical air. The scent of flowers, rain and damp earth was like a perfume to her. She loved the earthy sultriness of it.

Hot on Dallas's heels, she followed him down the unknown trail, realizing she would follow him just about anywhere. Then the sun showed itself for the first time since the storm had hit them. Dappled light exploded around her, lighting the rain forest into a myriad of greens. Flowers seemed to burst open under the warming heat of the sun and the forest steamed exotically around them.

Dallas reined up and pulled to a halt. Jimi followed suit.

"Look," she breathed, "it's so beautiful. You'd never know a storm had just wreaked havoc on us all."

"Nature is harsh and forgiving." He leaned over and placed his hand around her neck, tugging her to him.

"It's amazing." Jimi faced him, their lips so close.

"Yes, it is. I'm glad you came with me."

His kiss was almost sweet. Heart wrenching. And Jimi was moved beyond words. She answered his kiss, and for the first time since he'd come into her life, she realized this fling would be over soon. The thing was, it didn't feel like a *fling* anymore. She couldn't put her finger on exactly why, and it confused her.

"This is as far as we go on horseback. Ready for a bit of a hike?"

I'll follow you to the ends of the earth. But can I? Jimi pushed the conflicting thoughts away and decided to live in the moment.

"Lead the way, cowboy." Jimi swung down and landed on the soft forest ground easily. After looping the reins around a tree branch, she followed Dallas as he disappeared into the lush forest on a trail only he could see.

HEARING JIMI FOLLOWING him gave Dallas a sense of contentment. He was surprised how much his thoughts about her had shifted over the past days. He liked being with her. Not just sexually, which was without a doubt the best sex he'd had even in its frantic haste, but just in her presence. She was a handful to be sure. He liked that, and the last thing he wanted was to tame her.

He wanted to see her expression when she saw this special place. It wasn't on the regular tours. Tricky to get at and he preferred to keep it less traveled, so to speak.

"Keep to the path. This is an ecologically sensitive area and we like to keep it as untouched as possible."

"It's really quite beautiful. I wouldn't have expected such a lush place in this area."

"It's one of my favorite places on the ranch. Another few minutes and we'll be there."

Dallas reached back and took her hand when the path widened enough for them to walk abreast. He liked it when she curled her fingers around his hand. It felt good. Their time together was drawing to a close and he had no idea what would be coming next. If anything. He was going to make the most of being together with her. He knew she'd be leaving to go home after the wedding, and he would be left behind to take the ranch to the next level of business. And he had the mare ready to foal. His life was complicated. But being out here with her in nature seemed to take away all those worries. Shit, he was just making excuses. She was a city girl, and he knew she'd break his heart if he let it go too far.

"Oh, my," Jimi whispered, and clutched his hand tighter. "Breathtaking."

They emerged from the forest to the edge of a pool surrounded by lush ferns and flowers of all varieties, which clung to the black lava rock wall that horseshoed the pool. The sun poked through the tree canopy that seemed to arch over the water, embracing this very special place. Again they were bathed in sunny light.

Dallas was pleased to see the look of wonder on her face. Bringing her here had been a good idea after all.

"This is beautiful." Jimi walked forward and crouched at the edge of the pool, running her fingers through the clear water. "It's warm. I thought it would be chilly."

"It's our hot spring, or pond. There's some on the island, and we're fortunate to have one on our property. The others are public, but this one we've kept private."

"How is it heated?"

"Geothermal. From the volcano."

Jimi swished her hand around in the water. "I'd totally forgotten about the volcano." He chuckled and Jimi smiled. "I suppose not being from here would make it easy to forget about the volcano, but in actuality, how *could* you forget about it? You know, I'd be interested in seeing it." She turned to him. "Is that possible? Do they have tours?"

He nodded. "Yes, you can do a helicopter tour and see the crater, walk through a lava tube—"

"Seriously? Lava tubes? That would be an experience."

"Well, maybe we can do it after things calm down."

HE'S THINKING OF the future. When we're not stuck up here.
Jimi wasn't sure how to feel about that. But she

couldn't deny the flutter in her heart at the thought of
seeing him again after all this wedding drama was over.
She looked at him and smiled. "I'd like that."

He gave her a devilish grin and stepped toward her.
The look in his eyes dark and intense. Jimi was mesmerized and she stood up, waiting for him. Anxious to
see what he had on his mind.

No words. Just a look and the touch of his hands on her
shoulders, and then she was in his arms. Hers wrapped
around his neck, she pressed herself to his strength. She
tipped her head back, and her blood raced thicker, hotter
in her veins as his gaze roved over her face, lingering on
her mouth and then back up to her eyes.

"I never expected this to happen," she whispered.

"What to happen?" He smiled and she was so thoroughly enchanted, her eyes filled with unexpected tears.

"This. You. Here."

"Ah, I see. Well, I can say the same, *hemahema*."

Then his lips were on hers. His hands in her hair. His
body crushed to hers. His heat enveloped them, along
with the sounds of the forest they stood in. Jimi heard
every noise—the leaves, the wind in them, the water in
the pool, even the horses way off in the distance as they
stamped their hooves. Most important, she heard Dallas, the deep intake of his breath as his mouth moved
over hers. His tongue at her lips, pressing and asking
for entry. Entry she would never ever deny him.

Jimi moaned, opening her mouth. Her body flared
to life when his tongue swept inside seeking hers. She
met him and it was like he drew her into his body,
his soul. Engulfing her in his essence and very being.
Then all was silent as she became so in tune to him.

The thumping of his heart next to her breasts. Her own heart beating in frantic rhythm. The way he pulled her hair, deliciously demanding, forcing her head back. She clutched his shoulders, hanging on as if she might spin off the world he'd just tipped on its axis. Nothing had been normal since she'd met him the other day.

I don't ever want it to be normal again. A little voice spoke to her, whispering so quietly it was hard to hear until it became so loud she couldn't ignore it even if she wanted to.

DALLAS WAS GLAD he'd brought her here. Her response delighted him. He'd hoped she would like this special place as much as he did. Taking her in his arms and kissing her until she hung limp in his arms was becoming far too important to him. To feel her, taste her, smell her had become like a drug he'd become addicted to. She was working her way under his skin. He'd told himself for the time being that was fine. She'd be on her way after their unintended fling and it would be aloha for them, and then what? Be on their merry way with only memories to hold them?

He hated that thought and gripped her tighter, fisting his hand into her thick curls, pulling her head back with a determination and possessiveness he wanted her to feel. Dallas searched her mouth with his tongue, as if to imprint her, in case he never kissed her again. Despair at that very unsettling thought impaled him. He pushed her back until she was pinned between him and a tree. She didn't complain and clung to him as if her life depended on it.

I like that. I want her to depend on me. Dallas knew she was an independent woman with a business of her own. Could she ever truly depend on him? Or need him?

Her sweet, soft moans drove him to distraction. He wanted to take her here, now in the wild of his Hawaiian ranch. Just the two of them in the forest, with nothing but the sounds of nature to witness their loving.

A shrill ring made him start. It took a moment before Dallas realized his satellite phone had come to life at the most inopportune time. Normally he'd ignore it, not letting it interrupt them, but today he had to take the call, all things considered.

"Mmm," he murmured into her mouth before breaking the kiss. "I gotta take this."

Dallas gazed down at her face. His stomach tightened, and it reached right down into his balls. She was exquisite. Perfect. Her eyes closed, lips shiny and plump after his kissing, chest heaving with her rising passion made him regret his choice.

Keeping his hand pushed into her hair, Dallas juggled the phone with the other. "What?" he barked.

"It's Tucker. The river is low enough to get across now. We're packing up and ready to go by the time you ride back."

Sounded like his brother wasn't leaving room for discussion. In any event, the people would want to get back down to civilization anyhow. Dallas switched his gaze from looking off into the forest to Jimi. Her eyes were open and she was watching him.

"Yeah, see you soon," he told Tucker before ending the call. Jimi was looking at the pond, a wistful expression on her face. What was she thinking? "So, looks like we're no longer stranded."

"I gathered as much. That means we can leave." It wasn't a question, simply a statement. She turned to him and he was surprised to see a flash of sadness in her eyes. "The last few days have been very surreal, completely unexpected, exciting and strange, and I've had the time of my life. Even if I was scared out of my mind for the most part of it."

Dallas pulled her into a bear hug, kissing the top of her head. He liked how her arms slipped around his waist and held him tight. "I wouldn't have let anything happen to any of the guests." He wanted to say *to you*, but the words wouldn't come.

THE RIDE BACK down to the camp seemed to fly by. Jimi couldn't pull her attention from Dallas. He looked so damn good in the saddle, he was born to ride. He led the way back down the trail and she tried to take in the sights around her. The beauty of the island surrounded them and she wanted to absorb it all. Imprint it into her memory so she would never forget the experiences here.

The frenzy of the camp was palpable when they arrived. Dallas pulled up at the barn and dismounted, looping his reins over a post. Jimi followed suit and stroked her gelding's neck, watching all the activity around her. Dallas was immediately swarmed by the wranglers. Clearly he was boss hog here, and they all looked to him for guidance. He glanced at her, gave her a wink and shrugged his shoulder. She took it as an apology that he no longer had time to spend with her. She forced a smile even though her belly was in knots and nodded, watching as he walked into the barn.

Still petting the horse's neck, Jimi was surprised when he came back out of the barn a few seconds later.

"One of the hands will take care of the horse. You

might want to head over to your tent and make sure nothing is left behind. Then meet everyone down at the trucks." He glanced around and then swooped in for a quick kiss before turning and jogging back into the barn before Jimi could even process the kiss and the fact that he was gone.

She furrowed her brows, wondering why he acted so surreptitiously around her. She stroked the horse's nose, enjoying the silky warmth of his coat. She wasn't about to jump to conclusions where Dallas was concerned, because she had no claim over him anyway. Now that this debacle of a ranch trip was coming to a close, it likely meant their fling was over, as well. Her belly turned over and she felt a little ill at the thought. How could that be, though, after only a couple of days together? But she did have to admit they had been an amazing few days in so many ways.

Moments later a wrangler from the barn came out and she led her horse over to him.

"Thank you."

"It's my pleasure, ma'am. I'm so sorry about the weather."

"Don't be silly. You had nothing to do with that. Nobody did. It was just bad circumstance."

"Thank you. I hope you enjoy the rest of your stay in Hawaii."

The ranch hand led the horse into the barn. Jimi followed and looked into the building. It was hard to believe they'd spent the past couple of days taking refuge inside this place. Truth be told, she was glad now that it was over. Not the time spent with Dallas, though—she would never regret what they'd shared together. Roughing it had brought her crashing back to childhood memories that she'd worked so hard to forget. No one knew what the future held or what kind of hurdles would be thrown in their path, and these last few days had proved that.

Jimi glanced at the sky, glad to see the dark clouds were breaking up even more now. The blue sky was a welcome sight, and she had a flurry of excitement for the rest of her stay in Hawaii. Three days into a three-week stay, a well-deserved holiday she couldn't deny.

Finding her tent, she poked her head inside to see if anything had been left behind. There really wasn't much to forget. Her dress and shoes and purse must be already packed in the truck. The few items of borrowed clothing sat on the bed and she scooped them up, wanting to make sure they were returned to their rightful owners after they had been laundered at the hotel.

Hotel.

She glanced over her shoulder at the tent, clearly having taken a beating from the hurricane. It was so far from the five-star accommodations she was accustomed to that she actually laughed out loud. She'd adjusted quite well and enjoyed herself. Even with all the inconveniences. But she was eagerly looking forward to her suite. To be clean, pampered, in her own clothes. Jimi sighed, imagining a day at the spa.

Down at the trucks, everybody was loaded up, and she squished into the back of the cube van with the rest of the group.

"Is there any room for me?" she inquired, and gave a bright smile to the rest of the weather-battered crowd as she folded herself into a tiny little spot.

"You betcha, honey." An older woman slid over and

made room for her on a box. "We've all been pretty co-zied up the last few days—nothing like a little bit more togetherness."

Jimi laughed, as did the woman and the rest of the wedding guests. The excitement inside the truck was catchy, and everyone was chattering at the same time. The battery lanterns illuminated the inside.

"Okay, folks." One of the two ranch hands at the back of the truck called out, "We're going to lower the door and I hope you're all comfy in there. It's about a half-hour drive back down to the main house, providing the roads aren't too rough. You might get bounced around in there a bit, so if you need us just bang on the wall behind the cab." He pointed to the front. "Okay. You're all good? Closing the door."

Jimi looked out the opening, trying to find Dallas or at least catch a glimpse of him. Then the door slid shut, sealing them all off from the outside. It took a moment for Jimi's eyes to adjust to the gloom. She sighed and shook her head. This was the last kind of holiday experience she had ever expected in a million years.

9

Jimi paused in front of the door to her suite. She was booked into the Kou Suite at the Four Seasons Hualalai. Turning the key, she pushed the door and the cool, elegant rooms greeted her. She gasped. It was absolutely stunning. A complete opposite from where she'd spent the last few days.

Jimi stood in the middle of the living area and gazed around. It was the most beautiful hotel room she'd ever seen. The furniture and appointments were lovely and gave a wonderful tropical feel. Decorated in such a way that she truly felt she was in Hawaii. Unlike her recent accommodations in the barn.

Winged by two bedrooms, the living area was gracious and seemed huge the way it flowed openly to the lanai. Beyond that was the beach only steps from the railing and then the ocean. The bedroom on the left had two queen beds. She knew the other one on the right must be the master bedroom. The view from the king-size bed matched the living area's. Breathtaking.

Sliding doors led to the lanai, with trees nicely shading the lounge chairs covered with colorful pillows. She looked at the big bed, and it reminded her of the cot she'd shared with Dallas.

I wonder if we'll ever have a chance to share a large bed like that?

She shoved the thought aside and turned around. Another door led to what looked like a dressing room. She wandered in to the walk-in closet. Her suitcases sat inside. She'd completely forgotten about her lost bags and that in itself was a revelation. She opened a folded note on top of a chest of drawers.

"Your wedding dress is being pressed and will be returned shortly."

Thank God! She was dying to make sure it hadn't been damaged. Could she trust the hotel laundry to handle the dress appropriately? On a sudden urge she picked up the phone on the table behind her and pressed the button for her butler.

"Yes, Ms. Calloway."

"Hello. I'm calling about the wedding dress that was in my luggage. I found the note that said it had been taken to be pressed. I can't stress enough that this dress must not be damaged and utmost care must be taken with it."

"I can assure you, Ms. Calloway, it will be very carefully pressed."

Jimi let out a sigh of relief. "Thank you."

"My pleasure, Ms. Calloway. Please call if you require anything else."

"Thank you. Goodbye."

Relief flooded through her—the photo spread would be perfect. Because rather than the exquisite dress she'd designed being paraded around at a hoedown, it would be in a luxurious hotel. On the beach. Where it belonged, just like the rest of her clothes. The butler had unpacked and everything hung neatly or had been folded and tucked away in the drawers. She sighed and sent a silent thank-you for butler service. Everything would be done for her. Every whim, need and desire attended to before she even had a chance to think what exactly it was she wanted. Butlers, in her experience, read minds. It was their job and she'd never been disappointed with butlers.

Yet, for the first time, she was thinking twice about it. Jimi sighed and shoved the drawer shut. There was no joy. No excitement. Just meh. She thought about this for a moment and wondered why what would once have given her such pleasure didn't have the same luster. She continued on with her exploration of the rooms, trying not to dwell on her new unsettled feelings.

Just beyond the dressing room was a bathroom unlike anything she'd ever seen. A large glass-walled shower was on the left wall, with a double-sink vanity on the facing wall. A lovely deep bathtub, which could easily fit two people, on the right. What was even more stunning and totally unexpected was the glass wall behind the tub to a private, outside shower. It was a pity she had no one to share this opulence with.

Dallas.

She eyed the bathtub. A long soak in a bubble bath would be heaven and wash off the past few days. She remembered the brief moment they'd had together in the rain as the storm had eased. The only bathing had come from standing in the rain. The two of them, their faces turned up to the sky as they were drenched in the freshness of the rainfall. How he'd smoothed the hair out of her face, held her cheeks and kissed her in the rain, which had led to her frantically getting his clothes off and him stripping her. Until they were naked in nature.

Jimi shivered now, remembering the delicious feel of his hands sliding down her slick body until he had grasped her ass and lifted. She'd clung to him. Arms around his neck, legs circling his thighs like a vise as he drove his cock deep inside her. It hadn't taken long for her to come, nor him. Something about their lovemaking was so powerful, raw, it blew her mind. It was never gentle, or could really ever be called lovemaking. It was fucking with an abandon that was unlike her. A hot tingle ran down her spine... They'd not used a condom. She thought about that for a moment, and realized she wasn't all that concerned about it. Being with Dallas was the best thing that had ever happened to her. He'd taken her to places she'd never been and never wanted to leave.

She swiped the tear that hovered on the edge of her eyelid, something else that was new to her. This sense of tenderness and emotion that thoughts of him roused in her. No man had ever done that before. Perhaps because she never let them. Seeing how her mom had tried so hard for her dad's affection and never gotten it had burned a deep scar. Jimi wanted a man who would be her one and only, treat her special and not move on to someone else when or if he ever grew tired of her. It was something she'd be unable to control, unlike her business and career, which was hers and hers alone.

Jimi hugged herself as her body trembled, remembering his skillful touch. If she showered or bathed, she would be washing him off her, and she wasn't ready to do that yet. She wanted to hang on to her Dallas just a little bit longer.

She wandered back through the rooms thinking about him. Would she see him again? What was he doing? Was he thinking of her? She hadn't even had the chance to say goodbye to him once they got back down to the big house. The bus had been waiting to take everybody to the hotels and he was still up at the camp. It was all so hectic. Kicking off the borrowed boots, Jimi stepped across the tile floor out to the private lanai that ran the width of her suite, where she toed off the socks, also borrowed, and enjoyed the feel of the warm wood beneath her feet.

The view was spectacular. Frangipani and bougainvillea bushes in full bloom ringed the lanai and scented the air. Such a colorful assault on her eyes was almost painful, especially after the last few days in the gloomy, rain-darkened forest. Which seemed like a lifetime ago now. Dare she admit she missed it?

Leaning on the lanai railing, under the overhang of tropical trees, Jimi inhaled and gazed out at the beach just steps away. She couldn't get over how gorgeous everything was. She closed her eyes and listened to the waves. Jimi loved the sound of the surf. Maybe she'd been a mermaid in a previous life.

Opening her eyes, she looked up and down the beach, absolutely stunned by how beautiful it was. Past the

scent of frangipani, which she loved, was the scent of
the sand and sea. The earth. Nature. Heat from the sun.
The air so heavy and sultry with that special smell of
Hawaii, it was intoxicating. Gone was the aroma of
horse, leather, rain, wet earth…and Dallas. Her chest
clenched and she gripped the railing until the wave of
pain receded.

I miss him.

The sun dappled through the trees, splashing a ka-
leidoscope of greens and yellows across the lanai. But
she hardly noticed any of it, staring off and lost in the
vast expanse of the sea beyond. She thought about everything on her plate when she got home. All the work,
the deadlines. She would have to make sure she rested
and recharged her batteries so she would be in top form.

"Well, now what?" Jimi murmured. "Everything almost seems so pointless without Dallas. Will I really be
able to relax and basically do nothing?" She doubted it,
especially with so much that was suddenly weighing on
her mind. She was waiting to hear about the revamped
plans for the wedding. So there was that.

She sighed, fascinated by the way the water and sky
merged on the distant horizon. It only made her think of
the first night at the camp, before the storm, at the ridge
watching the sunset. And…their first kiss, passionate,
demanding, breathtakingly glorious. Jimi shivered, and
a sense of longing for *him* filled her. Which led into remembering their passion in the tent. She hugged herself
as desire ran hot and thick in her blood.

*Everything circles back to him. Every thought and
memory.*

Would she ever see him again? Would she ever stop reliving their passion? They hadn't exchanged phone numbers or made any future plans. It had finished as quickly as it had begun. A fling. A wonderful, sexy, shiver-inducing fling.

Not used to the feeling of desperation growing deep inside her, she wasn't quite sure how to deal with it. It was like something had been cut out of her, leaving a gaping, raw-edged wound that would never heal. Maybe it was best it had ended like it had. Without any good-byes or promises that would be broken.

She turned her back to the sea, and somehow that seemed to symbolize turning her back on the glorious time with Dallas. She had to let him go. Being with him had been so great. Easy and wonderful. And she hadn't thought of her business once.

She stood up and processed that. Not good. If he could be so distracting, it was concerning. It didn't mean she had to forget him. If anything, she had to give him thanks for accepting her as she was and still liking her. He'd cracked open her shell enough for her to see the light on the other side. The opportunities. The possibilities. It was up to her if she was going to sink or swim.

And right now she had to get her house in order. Make sure the dress was perfection, and reach out to the home office and ensure everything for the photo shoot was on point. Once she did this, and made sure it was all on track, only then could she relax for a well-earned vacation.

BY THE TIME Dallas got back down to the big house all the guests had been shuttled away. He was in a foul, angry mood that he'd missed the opportunity to say a proper goodbye to Jimi. He hadn't really wanted to say goodbye at all, more of an aloha until he saw her again. She hadn't left any notes for him, or a phone number, or which hotel she was staying at. How was he supposed to interpret that? Was she done with him? Was that it—just a holiday fling? He let out a sigh. It hurt and he felt a little bit burned by it. The wedding was to be over the next few days and they'd both be there. He could find out then.

There's too much to do at this point to go gallivanting off in search of her. They had a whole lot of repair to do after the storm. Plus, he wanted to make sure he could help Matt and Diana in any way possible.

Samantha had handled it all pretty well, in his opinion. She'd kept her calm. The wedding guests had been entertained to the best of her ability under the circumstances. He was thankful everybody had come out of the situation unharmed.

He smiled thinking of how they'd all been pretty good sports. Especially Jimi. Once the storm had subsided, she'd seemed to relax even more, and he'd enjoyed being around her. It almost had him thinking they could have dinner or something before she went home. *Home.* He frowned. He'd gotten caught up and forgotten she was a mainlander. A vacationer.

Dallas kicked off his boots outside the door to the mudroom. He could hear voices and slapped his hands on his jeans to get rid of any extra dust before going into the house proper.

"Dallas!" A female voice hollered for him. "Get your butt in here."

Larson could really be demanding when she wanted to. His sister was a spitfire challenge that would give any man a run for his money.

"I'm coming. Hold your horses." He stopped in the kitchen, opened the stainless-steel fridge and pulled out a beer. "Anyone want a brew?" he called out.

"Yeah, I'll take one."

"Me, too."

"Just bring five and one for yourself," Larson shouted from the great room.

Dallas grabbed five bottles in one hand and pulled out a bag of chips from the pantry. He'd had the kitchen redone a few years ago. A chef's dream. He couldn't cook, which made him wonder why he'd had such a fantastic kitchen put in here.

I wonder if Jimi likes to cook. He sighed, wondering how many times she would pop into his head.

The great room was just beyond the kitchen. The vast windows ran two stories high and gave a spectacular view of the ranch and the rolling landscape down to the sea beyond. It was one of the rare sightings of the ocean on the property.

Even though they were in Hawaii, the room held a very Western appeal. He was useless at decorating, so he'd hired a designer to combine Western and Hawaiian decor. He was happy with the end result. It was a big house, built by his great-grandfather almost two hundred years ago, so it had desperately needed some updating and expansion. He still couldn't believe that HGTV wanted to do an episode here.

Larson, Tucker, Diana, Matt and Sam were all looking really comfy on the heavy leather couches.

"Here." He tossed the bag of chips to Tucker and handed each one a beer before dropping into the big armchair that he'd claimed as his own. "So. Drama's all over."

Sam sat up and placed her beer bottle on the coffee table. "It sure is. I certainly hope I never have to go through something like that again."

"But you did great, babe." Tucker was quick to compliment her. She tossed him a cheeky smile that Dallas noticed.

"You did, Sam, you really did. I don't know what I would've done had I been the coordinator. But under the circumstances I think it all went off really well." Larson was quick to defend her friend and grabbed the bag of chips from Tucker. "Don't eat them all."

"There's more in the cupboard." Tucker rebutted her.

"Then go get some for yourself." Larson held the chips away from him.

"Guys, come on. I'm exhausted," Tucker complained.

"So." Dallas turned to Matt and Diana and asked, "What's going to happen with the wedding now?"

"We're still not a hundred percent sure, but we have to make a decision pretty fast," Matt replied. "I think we've actually decided to leave that up to Samantha to iron out. Just keep Thursday night open."

Matt turned and smiled at Samantha. She raised her eyebrows and shrugged her shoulders. "All I can say is

I'm glad we reserved the venues for the second reception party and we're just rejuggling a few little things."

Diana leaned forward and grabbed a beer, holding it out to Matt while he twisted off the cap. "Agreed, but I don't think I want to have a buffet on the beach. I'd rather it be served. Everybody's been making do over the past few days, so it would be nice to go a little more posh." Diana gave Sam a big smile. "But I'm leaving it all up to you, honey. That's why we pay you the big bucks."

"If you leave it all up to me, just go and enjoy yourself at the resort and stay out of my hair—it'll be perfect."

"So party time is coming, then, I presume," Tucker asked and grabbed a beer.

"You bet your ass." Matt put his arm around Diana's shoulders and hugged her tight. "I think we've had enough of roughing it. Time to spoil my bride."

Dallas leaned back in his chair and rested his ankle on his knee. Watching the rest of them banter back and forth was comforting and he felt all the tension seep out of him. Knowing he had no further responsibilities until the next group of guests arrived in a week was heaven. He could focus back on the working side of the ranch and take a few days to chill. Being responsible for all those guests during a hurricane was not his idea of fun—the only fun was the time he'd spent with Jimi.

"So I guess all of your wedding guests have been deposited at various hotels?" he asked.

"Yes, most of them are at the Four Seasons Hualalai, where we plan to have our wedding and reception. But some are staying at other hotels and B and Bs," Diana informed him.

Dallas tipped his head back and took a swig from the beer bottle, wondering where Jimi was staying. But he wasn't about to ask. He wasn't ready to let that cat out of the bag yet. He'd just have to wait and hope to see her at the wedding. Two days away.

10

JIMI WAS EXCITED. After having lunch with Diana yesterday and handing over the wedding gown and making last-minute touch-ups, Jimi could barely contain herself. Diana had fallen in love with the gown, gushing over it, and Jimi was so thankful. It meant her design was a hit. She had been able to create what a bride wanted.

Finally Matt and Diana were getting married! A personalized note had arrived requesting her presence at the Wedding Tree to witness their exchange of wedding vows. Reception to follow later on the Moana Terrace.

Not only was she psyched about the wedding, she wondered if she'd see Dallas again. He might not have been invited to the wedding. Oh, how she hoped that wasn't the case.

After studying the resort map, she'd had an idea where to go and decided to walk up the beach. For the first time since arriving in Hawaii she'd decided to get herself all dolled up and had spent the last couple of hours getting ready. Picking out just great shoes to go with the perfect dress. Artfully arranging her hair after straightening it ruthlessly. She applied makeup, the first time in days, and hardly recognized the woman reflected in the mirror. This had been her normal routine prior to coming to Hawaii. A morning didn't pass without Jimi spending it before the mirror. The application had been rather exhausting and not as satisfying as she thought it would be and, she admitted to herself, a waste of time. Maybe it was time to rethink some things.

The boardwalk that ran the length of the beach would've been the best way for her to get to the Wedding Tree, no sand in her Jimmy Choos, but she wanted—no, needed—to feel the sand next to her skin again. Jimi pulled off her shoes and let them dangle from her fingers. She stepped down into the sand with a sigh. It was warm, as was the breeze coming off the ocean. It played with her hair, threatening to pull it from the clips she'd used to set it. If it came down, it came down. Whatever. It felt so right walking barefoot in the sand. It wasn't a long walk, and there were cute little signs along the way stuck into the sand that had I Do painted on them with an arrow pointing the way to go.

Jimi followed the crescent-shaped, white-sand beach to an outcropping of black lava rock. Trees atop it arched over a lovely arbor decorated in beautiful tropical flowers. Teak chairs, with colorful throw pillows, fanned in rows from the arbor shrouded with tropical flowers. Pink flower petals had been cast over the sand leading up to the altar. It was just stunning.

Jimi joined the guests mingling about. Many she recognized from the camp, and she searched all the faces for Dallas. But there was no sign of him. The couple she'd seen the night of the hurricane smiled at her and she walked over to them. A beautiful and graceful hula dancer swayed to the music played by a duo done up in Hawaiian finery. The sweet, musical notes filled the air.

"Hi. This is a far cry from what we've experienced the last few days. This is so lovely," Jimi commented.

The woman looked up at her with a puzzled expression on her face. "Have we met?"

Jimi felt a little embarrassed that the woman didn't recognize or remember her. "Oh, yes. We were up at the camp together during the hurricane."

"Oh, my! I barely recognized you. You look gorgeous. I guess this means you've gotten your suitcases back."

"Yes, they were waiting for me here when I arrived. It sure does seem odd to get all dressed up after roughing it."

"Well, I certainly wouldn't have recognized you. What a transformation." The woman smiled, but, rather than making Jimi feel good about her appearance, it almost made her feel phony. But she sensed the woman wasn't deliberately trying to make her feel that way. "It was an experience, I must say. I don't think we got the chance to introduce ourselves up there. I'm Lana and this is my fiancé, Grant."

"I'm Jimi. Nice to finally know your names. Are you friends of the bride or groom?"

Grant answered, "The groom. And you?"

"The bride. We went to college together and our lives took us in different directions. Now, that accent, don't tell me… South African?"

Lana laughed and clapped her hands together. "It's not often people can pick out accents, especially the South African one. Everybody thinks it's Australian."

"Well, one of the companies I used to work for had employees from around the world, so I became familiar with different accents."

Lana took Grant's hand, and Jimi didn't miss the look of affection he gave her. The love they showed each other was written all over them. Jimi envied the couple.

"You have a date set?" Jimi inquired.

"We have a few set aside—it all depends on Sam," Lana told her.

"I've got to hand it to her after the way she handled everything during the hurricane. And then pulling this off..." Jimi waved her hand around. "This is spectacular."

The strangest sound filled the air. A low deep hum that was almost haunting. It sent shivers along Jimi's spine, and she turned around to find the source of the sound.

"Aw, that's so cool," Lana whispered. "A conch blower."

Standing just beyond the trees on an outcrop of black lava, a man dressed in native Hawaiian costume held a conch shell to his mouth, with his head tilted toward the setting sun. The long, low moan coming from the shell filled her with a sense of wonder. She presumed it was a call to ceremony as the rest of the guests began to make their way to the carefully placed chairs.

Jimi felt a touch on her shoulder and turned. Her heart dropped to see it was Lana. She'd been hoping to see Dallas standing there, so she tried to hide her disappointment.

"We'll see you after the ceremony at the reception."

"Okay, it was nice chatting with you." Jimi followed the couple as they walked to their seats. She couldn't get over how lovely the wedding decor was. The little candles and glass holders were tucked into the stand beside the chair closest to the aisle, and flowers and seashells ringed the base. She was eager to see Diana in her dress. An empty chair under the arch of an over-hanging tree was the perfect spot for her. It was out of the way and in the shadows.

Glancing around, Jimi was enchanted. The sun was slowly setting, and cast a beautiful golden glow tinged with pink across the sand, making the pink flowers pop to life with vibrant color. The black lava rocks couldn't possibly be any blacker and even the surf seemed to pause in its ebb and flow, as if waiting for the bride and groom to say their vows.

The music faded away and the Hawaiian conch blower did a long, mournful sound. A very Hawaiian-looking officiant took his place under the flower-covered arbor. Jimi turned in her chair to see Matt approach. He was very handsome in his white pants and tropical shirt, which matched the flowers decorating the venue. She took the opportunity to cast a quick look around, and her heart dropped. There was still no sign of Dallas.

Oh well. Maybe it was just a fling after all.

The crowd drew in a collective gasp when Diana emerged from behind a gauzy curtain that had been erected to shield her from the wedding guests. She was absolutely gorgeous. Her hair, pulled back on one side, had a spray of flowers braided into the strands. Her gown sparkled and shimmered as she walked toward the aisle. The fabric of her wedding dress floated around her while, at the same time, it clung to her curves, accentuating her figure and ending in soft scallops just above her ankles. Perfection. Jimi breathed a sigh of relief that it had all ended well. She was barefoot, which was no surprise at all to Jimi. If ever there was a misplaced flower child, it was Diana. Born forty years too late.

A beautiful song began, and the crowd stood. Jimi recognized the notes as the "Hawaiian Wedding Song." It was wonderfully haunting, and a shiver rippled along her flesh. She watched Diana walk up the aisle of sand, scattered with flower petals, toward her groom. The simple elegance of the wedding ceremony touched Jimi very deeply. Emotions swelled inside her as they exchanged their vows and, to her surprise, tears spilled from her eyes. Not one to usually cry, she did now. Would she ever be a happy bride full of love? Did she want this? *Yes, I think I do.*

The officiant raised his hands as Diana and Matt turned to face the wedding guests.

"Please stand as I introduce Mr. and Mrs. Scott."

Jimi rose with the rest of the group and clapped happily. She was smiling and crying, just like Diana. The couple looked so happy, and Jimi was thrilled for them.

Just before they started their walk back up the aisle, they stopped and Matt raised his hand.

"Thank you for experiencing the last few days with us. I'm glad the weather has improved and that you were all able to join us on our special day. No more roughing it, so please make your way over to the Moana Terrace, where you shall be wined and dined and serenaded so you can dance the night away." He took Diana's hand and placed it into the crook of his elbow. "My bride and I are going to have the obligatory photographs taken and we will see you in about an hour. Mahalo."

As they passed, Diana blew Jimi a kiss and winked at her. Jimi smiled and nodded, swiping a lone tear as it slipped from her eye. She was thunderstruck when the pain in her heart made her realize she wished it was her walking down the aisle. Married. Yes, suddenly she felt the burning urge for a commitment. It was something she'd not ever considered before. Her business was too important, and marriage would only get in the way of that.

"Would it really?" Jimi asked herself. How would she ever know if she didn't at least entertain the idea. "Only thing is, I have no man in my life I'd even consider marrying." *Except maybe one.*

Then her vision blurred as she watched Diana and Matt walk away, only to refocus seeing herself and Dallas as the bride and groom.

"What?" Jimi mumbled, and blinked. Obviously her eyes *and brain* were playing tricks on her. But the image of the two of them walking down the aisle as husband and wife, gazing adoringly at each other, was seared into her brain.

"Mr. and Mrs., um…yeah…that's a positive sign. I don't even know his last name."

"Damn!" Dallas swore. He hated being late for anything. Slowing the truck in the parking lot of the Four Seasons, he grimaced when the tires squealed a bit as he swung the half ton into a spot under a banyan tree. The last few days had certainly been a challenge, right from the start of Matt and Diana's glamping disaster to almost losing the foal earlier today.

It had been a sixty-mile drive on a two-lane road that made for slow going from the ranch. He'd missed the wedding ceremony and was coming in well after the dinner and speeches. Likely people would be leaving the party about now, but at least he could put in an appearance, however short it might be. Plus, he hoped he'd see Jimi.

Everything had gone on hold when his phone rang with Larson's panicked voice on the other end. It had been a grueling day and, thankfully, the foal and the mare were just fine. He'd taken a risk shipping her to Kentucky and having her bred to American Prince, then returned home here for the birth. Dallas hated to see the sad side of ranching. Baby deaths.

He ran his hand through his still-damp hair. Showering and dressing at the barn facilities after the veterinarian had left helped shave off some time. Which reminded him—he'd forgotten his shaving kit. Running a hand over the stubble on his jaw, he hoped it wasn't too noticeable.

He jogged through the parking lot, looking for signs for the Moana Terrace. He knew that was near the beach, but this was a big resort—and a gorgeous one at that. Especially at night with the torches illuminating the paths and twinkling lights everywhere. He headed toward the lobby, knowing he'd be directed properly from there.

This was the first time he'd ever been at this resort and he was impressed with how nice it was. Not a glaring monstrosity but graciously built into the land around it, enhancing the natural beauty. He nodded as he walked along the torch-lit path, liking what he saw. Soon he was closer to the sea and the entrance to the Moana Terrace. It sounded like they were having a rollicking good time inside. He climbed the steps to the second floor.

"Dallas!" Diana spied him as he entered and rushed to envelop him in a big hug. "I'm so glad you were able to make it. Is the baby okay?"

He'd sent them a text earlier telling them he might be late and why.

"Yes. We have a little colt, and, hopefully, he'll be just like his daddy once he grows up."

Diana clapped her hands. "I'm so happy for you. It's a big step to get into Thoroughbred racing."

"Don't I know it."

Matt made his way over to them after extricating himself from the guests on the dance floor doing the Time Warp.

"So, twinkle toes," Dallas teased him, "having a great day?"

"You bet. The best," Matt replied, and clapped Dallas on the back. "So glad you made it. There's going to be food later, so you can chow down if you're hungry."

"Great. I'm starved."

"Hey, I'm sure I can get you something else. You don't have to wait until later," Diana said, and was off before he could tell her not to worry about it.

He glanced around, looking at all the guests. He wondered if Jimi had come. He sought out her wild mane of blond curls, figuring he'd be able to spot her in the crowd without any trouble at all. He didn't see her and was disappointed.

"Looks like Diana has rustled up some food for you," Matt informed him as his bride returned, carefully balancing a plate and a cocktail.

"Here, sit down and enjoy. It's time for us to take care of you, after all you did for us during the storm." She leaned down and kissed him on the cheek. "Thank you."

Dallas actually felt his cheeks heat up with a touch of embarrassment. "All in a day's work. I'm just glad everything came off without too much of a hitch." He gazed around.

"Are you looking for someone?"

"Just seeing if all the faces are familiar." He wasn't about to tell her he was looking for Jimi. He wasn't ready for the storm of questions that would set off.

"I see." Diana's voice held a humorous tone. Dallas swung his gaze to look at her. He tipped his head sideways, knowing she was dying to ask him something. "But I don't believe you."

"You don't?" he drawled, crossing his arms over his chest. "Why not?"

"I saw you two up there. Even though you guys were trying to hide it, I felt your connection, but I wasn't really sure how far it had gone." She regarded him as if waiting for him to spill his guts. Not likely. "Hmm, if only you'd arrived a few minutes earlier."

Yes, indeed. If only… His heart tumbled in his chest when he saw a woman on the other side of the dance floor. Moving his head to see through the sea of people, he couldn't tell if it was Jimi or not. Blond head with hair sleeked back, graceful, but no curly hair and way too tall. Through the heads bopping up and down and arms waving to the song "YMCA," it was hard to see her features. She had a glass of wine in her hand and was leaving the terrace. Definitely taller than Jimi, and rather than a wild riot of curls, her hair was straight as a die and pulled back into a tight bun. She appeared far too different from Jimi's earthy, wild-child appeal. Dallas sighed and finished the beer. Time to go.

11

"RENT A BIKE," they'd said. "You'll like it," they'd said. "It's not hard," they'd said. "You'll get to see the beauty of the island," they'd said. "It's good exercise," they'd said.

Well, *they* were full of shit, in her opinion. The bike she'd rented from the hotel was a good one, but it had been years since she'd pedaled anywhere. Least of all along this long road with hills and valleys and heat and wind. Maybe this had been a mistake. Even though the bike lane was fairly wide, the cars flew by with a gust of wind that almost knocked her off the bike. As much as she wanted to stop and rest and grab a drink of water, she was afraid to.

One thing Jimi had to admit, though, was the fantastic view. She was breathless, not only by the effort of riding but by the spectacular scenery she was riding through. The land was very rugged and raw, hardly any plants growing. Almost like a tropical desert. The wind whipped off the ocean, as well, buffeting her along with the blow-by of the cars. She hung on to the handlebars until her knuckles turned white.

I'm going to do this thing!

Getting more active after spending such a rugged time camping had been her new resolution. Even though New Year's was only a couple of months behind her, there was no reason she couldn't make a new vow today.

The crystal blue of the sea to her left was absolutely stunning. So brilliant under a matching blue sky. Jimi coasted down a shallow grade, glad there were no cars flying by her. She could take a moment to relax, and she sat a little taller on the bike seat.

"Oh! Whales!" she shouted, her words getting swept away by the wind. She'd always wanted to go whale watching. And here she was riding a bike along a highway on the Big Island of Hawaii with these magnificent creatures putting on a show for her. Jimi watched them more than she watched the road. If she were to die now it couldn't have happened in a more spectacular place.

She was going at a fairly quick pace down the hill, with still no cars for the time being. So she watched the whales and when one breached, crashing back down into the water and sending a spray of sea foam into the air, Jimi gasped and held her breath at the wonder of it. Even though they were quite a distance from her, she could see them clearly.

The front wheel of her bicycle made a sudden jolt. She let out a cry and held on to the handlebars, trying to control the wheel, but the vibration coming up through the wheel into the handlebars threw her off balance. Jimi pulled on the brakes, trying to control the bicycle as it skidded out of the bike lane and onto the gravel shoulder. The loose stones grabbed the tires and spun the bike around. Trying to keep from falling onto the sharp stones, Jimi braced her feet to take the impact as the bike flipped out of her control. She did her best to vault away from the bike to keep from tumbling with it. She scampered to keep her balance, and her feet slid out from under her and she landed on one knee. This time she let out a proper scream at the pain of her flesh being torn on the knifelike rocks. She stopped for a second, blinked and caught her breath, then looked around to see if anybody had seen her fall. Thankfully, there were no cars bearing down on her. It took a moment to gather her wits about her, and she stood up, brushing herself off.

Jimi bent down to look at her knee. It needed a good cleaning and a bandage.

"Well, this is brilliant." She put her hands on her hips. "How typical. Cars breezing past me the whole way, and when I actually need somebody to be driving by, there's not a soul."

She looked around for the bike. After walking over to it, she grabbed the handlebars and hefted it upright. The front tire was flat. Of all frigging things to happen.

"Now, how can we get out of this one?" She'd been riding for almost an hour. Which meant the hike back to the hotel would be at least double that. She looked up at the sky. "Well, it's going to be a long, hot hike back."

She wasn't really surprised that no one stopped to see if she needed help as she walked the bike back in the direction of the hotel. She wasn't angry, either. She was just going to take it in stride. What else could she do? A small roadway led off to what appeared like a scenic lookout below. She hadn't noticed that when she'd first passed by. If circumstances had been different, she would have liked to go for a look. Likely there wasn't any phone down there, either. Why she hadn't thought to bring her cell phone was beyond her. And very stupid, especially under the circumstances.

She turned around when she heard tires crunching on stones as a vehicle pulled up behind her. So there were Good Samaritans in Hawaii after all. A big pickup truck stopped just shy of her and the driver's door opened.

"Jimi?"

She peered into the glaring sun as a tall man stepped from the truck. Her belly did a flip-flop.

No way—what are the odds of him driving by out here?

"Dallas? What are you doing out here?" Jimi dropped the bike and walked over to him. "What are you, like a knight in shining armor that materializes out of nowhere when needed?"

You can be my knight in shining armor anytime.

He threw back his head and laughed. "Well, here I am. What happened to you and why are *you* out here all by yourself?"

"Well, I decided I was going to get a bit of exercise, and people were telling me I should go cycling." She turned and waved her hand at the bike. "Looks like it was a good idea, huh?"

"What the hell happened? Are you okay?" The look of concern on his face warmed her, and she liked that feeling.

"I have no idea. The tires suddenly burst and I went flying off onto the shoulder. I scraped my knee, but I'll be fine." She cocked her head to the side and smiled at him. "No, really, though, why are you here? It just seems so crazy that we bump into each other out here in the middle of nowhere."

Dallas walked over to the bike and picked it up as if it were as light as a matchstick. He tossed it into the back of the truck. "It's common for flats along here, you know. They should have told you that. Anyway, I was in Hawi with my brother—he has a business there—and I decided that I was going to come and find you at the resort. I guess my timing was pretty good."

"Couldn't be better. Where's Hawi?"

He thumbed behind him. "About thirty miles that way. How far were you planning to ride this bike anyway?"

She shrugged her shoulders and pursed her lips. "I don't know. I hadn't really given it much thought other than just going thataway." She pointed in the same direction that Dallas had come from.

"Well, you have any plans right now? Other than taking care of that knee."

Dallas took her elbow, and a tingle rushed up her arm, igniting all of her nerve endings. He led her around to the passenger side of the truck and opened the door. She turned to face him, and stared up at him. Even through the dull ache in her knee, his presence had her body remembering every touch and kiss they'd shared in the days before. She wanted it again. Craved it. Craved *him*.

"Well, the Hawaiian gods must be shining down on me right now. Because I'm so glad you were driving by." She chewed her lip, trying to decide if she should say what she so desperately wanted to tell him.

But she didn't have time because he grasped her shoulders and pulled her toward him until their bodies were a hairbreadth apart. She swore the air between them crackled with an electric charge. Jimi was breathless as he lowered his face to hers. Was he going to kiss her? If he didn't, she'd bloody well make it happen herself.

His voice was low, like hot honey slipping around her. "I've not been able to get you out of my head."

She gasped and slid her hands around his waist. "Me, neither. When I didn't hear from you, I figured that was it. And you weren't at the wedding yesterday, a-and—"

"I was at the wedding. You weren't there. I never saw you." His fingers gripped her arm tightly and she welcomed the bite of pain. He made her feel alive, making her realize how she'd been just sleepwalking through her days for so long. "I didn't get there till late, though, and everybody was dancing by that time."

Jimi was puzzled. "I left just as the dancing was really ramping up. I was hoping to see you there, too, and when I didn't... I went back to my room."

Jimi took the bicycle helmet off. Dallas reached up and fingered the ponytail. "Your hair is straight."

"What an odd thing to say. I straightened it yesterday for the wedding."

"I've only ever seen you with curly hair."

"I don't understand. Why are you talking about my hair?"

Dallas smiled, and it was infectious. Jimi couldn't help returning it.

"It was you I saw last night." Gently he pulled the tie

from her hair so that it cascaded around her shoulders and blew in the wind off the sea. "You had it pulled back into a bun last night, right?"

"Yes. But why—"

"I didn't recognize you. You look so completely different all dressed up, not at all like I'm used to. You must've had on some killer high heels, because you were way taller than everybody else."

"I did. It's funny you say you didn't recognize me, because another couple from up at the camp didn't, either." Jimi shook her head, coming to an even greater realization. "You know, my whole adult life revolves around makeup and fashion and hair. But being here, looking like this…" She looked down at herself in the shorts and tank top and waved her hand up and down her body. "Makes you wonder what it's all for."

"While I didn't say you didn't look good last night— just that I didn't recognize you—I will tell you this… You look mighty fine right now, and good enough to eat."

Jimi laughed out loud, delighted with this turn of events. Her laughter was quickly silenced by Dallas's lips. She breathed him in, closed her eyes and let herself get lost in the magic of his kiss. His hands slid up her back and into her hair, lightly pressing against her skull as if he'd never let her go.

She clung to him, the burning in her knee forgotten as a new fire started up deep inside her. She thrust her hips forward, and he pushed into her, his erection hard and insistent next to her belly.

Jimi tugged his shirt from the waistband of his jeans. She needed to feel him. Wanted to crawl inside him and

have him wrap his strength around her. She pushed her
hands underneath his shirt, loving the feel of his muscles, like the strongest steel. Safe. Powerful. Protecting.

His tongue found hers, and tangled as he deepened
the kiss. Their bodies remembered each other, even after
only spending a few days together. She craved him like
a starved woman. Standing here under the hot Hawaiian
sun as cars sped by them in Dallas's arms was the only
place on earth she wanted to be.

Jimi was losing control. She wanted this man in the
worst way, and if he tossed her in the back of the truck
right now and ripped her clothes off her, she wouldn't stop
him. He groaned into her mouth before lifting his head
from her. Cupping her cheeks in his powerful hands, he
stared into her eyes. Jimi looked back at him, so aroused
she was barely able to draw a breath. Her breasts ached,
nipples hard and needing attention from him so badly.
Her thighs trembled and she leaned against him for support. Her body was oh so ready for him.

"D-Dallas." She whispered his name. "T-take me…"

"Exactly what I was thinking, too." He placed a gentle kiss on her lips. "Hop in the truck. Oh, and the first-
aid kit is in the glove box. Do your knee."

"Oh yes, I'd almost forgotten." Jimi found the kit, and
while she was fixing her knee up, she asked, "Where
can we go?"

"Anywhere you want, *hemahema*."

She smiled when he said the Hawaiian word for
clumsy. The word he'd called her the day they first met.

"I don't care where you take me. But wherever it is,

it better have a comfortable bed. I don't want to see another cot for the rest of my life."

"Then I know just the place."

DALLAS COULDN'T BELIEVE the coincidence of seeing her
on the highway. Now he had to think fast and figure
out how he was going to talk—*seduce*—her into staying with him for a couple of days. This time in luxury
and not all wet and, well… He wanted to try to impress
her, show her he was more than a *paniolo*.

She sat quietly in the truck looking out the window.
His captive. He smiled, liking her quiet presence beside
him. Dallas stole a glance. He highly doubted she knew
how alluring she was. He liked her like this. Fresh, natural, even sweaty and flushed from her bicycle ride, she
was amazingly sexy to him. Did she know it?

Dallas had been missing her since the end of the
glamping trip and hadn't realized just how much until
now. He would whisk her away to his cliff-side home
on the east shore just south of Hawi. His retreat. His
haven. He rarely took people to it, preferring to keep it
private and the world from creeping in. Now he wanted
to shut out the world from his private escape, except for
one person—Jimi.

"We're going to stop along the way. Grab some food
and something for you to wear."

"But I didn't bring any money," Jimi replied.

"My treat." Dallas smiled at her.

"I don't know about that." Jimi was concerned. "I
can't have you buying my clothes. I have plenty back
at my hotel. Why don't we just go back and get them?"

Dallas shook his head. "Nope. I have you now and I'm not letting you go anytime soon."

Money wasn't an issue; nor did he expect her to pay him back. He let it slide and decided to worry about it later if she brought it up. He was still reluctant to be completely open about his financial status. The fact that they were getting along so well, without that hanging over their heads, was a positive sign. She didn't appear greedy or money hungry, which led him to believe she could be independently wealthy. Not that he was worried about her paying him back. It made him wonder again just how independent she was. And what, if anything, could make her consider living outside New York City. This island was nothing like the bright lights and big city.

But he liked the way she smiled at his comment. His blood rushed a little hotter thinking of the next few days he hoped to have with her.

"You'll like this store," he told her. "We can pick up pretty much anything your little heart desires."

"It sounds like a great place. Are there clothing stores there?"

"Yep, formal wear to beachwear."

"I think I'm preferring beachwear these days. Enough of formal wear." She cast him a sideways glance with a smile.

He knew she was referring to the wedding, where she hadn't seen him and he hadn't recognized her.

"Well, there's plenty of that. And, quite frankly, I'd rather you have no clothes on."

She laughed. He liked her seductive tone and the way his body responded to her. As if she were part of him, he felt her energy like waves flowing over and inside him. So wild, unpredictable and, yes, difficult. A challenge. He knew deep in his soul that she would challenge him every step of the way, even if she didn't know she was doing it. And yet more surprising was Dallas realized at this moment how much he wanted that in a woman.

SITTING BESIDE DALLAS as they drove down the highway was heaven. She'd been just as shocked as he by their chance meeting on the highway. In fact, she was quite lucky he'd driven by; otherwise, she'd have a two-hour hike back to the resort. The shopping trip was a delightful interlude, and it was way too easy to forget her life back home. She felt a little unsettled at that and was determined more than ever to pay him back, which she told him.

Jimi opened the window and inhaled deeply. She didn't want air-conditioning—she wanted the Hawaiian air. To smell it. Feel the softness of it around her.

"This is lovely. It's a different landscape from the other side of the island."

"Yes, it's more tropical and also quite rocky at the same time. Of course, it's all lava rock."

She nodded. "It wasn't really what I expected Hawaii would be. I always imagined it would be flowers everywhere, palm trees, white-sand beaches, just a tropical paradise."

"Hawi is like that, and parts of each island have their lushness. This is the youngest of all the Hawaiian Islands, in geologic terms anyway, but in our terms it's old." He smiled.

"I'd love to see the volcano."

"Well, maybe we'll take a trip down there. We can walk through a lava tube."

"Love to! But how can you walk in lava tubes? Isn't that dangerous?"

He laughed, but it didn't make Jimi feel embarrassed. She laughed with him. It was so easy to be with this man. There was no pretense, just happiness.

"They're old lava tubes. And it's just a short stretch, but it gives you the idea of what they're like. It's quite something, really. To think that these tubes you're walking in were full of molten lava rushing from the volcano to the ocean."

"This island really is dynamic. Always growing and changing," Jimi commented. "I didn't take geology, but I worked in that firm when I was younger that gave me an idea of tectonics, earth sciences and so forth. But volcanoes are scary."

"Why are they scary?"

She snorted. "You're asking that question? It's like you're living on a bomb about to explode."

They arrived at Queens' MarketPlace and he parked the truck. The heat from the parking lot was stifling, and the cool interior of the grocery store was a welcome relief. She was in awe.

"Fabulous store," Jimi exclaimed. "It sort of reminds me of Whole Foods. Although I hardly ever shop there 'cause it's way too snobby." She looked at Dallas and raised her eyebrows. "So, do you cook?"

He laughed out loud. "If you call making toast and slicing tomatoes to put on it 'cooking,' then yes. No, I don't cook well. I'm the guy that grabs a bowl of cereal or whatever's handy in the fridge. But don't get me wrong. I do like a good meal and appreciate people who can cook."

"Well, if you don't cook, then how do you know about this store, and why would you come here?"

"Look around. I can get anything I want in here. See over there? How could a man ever starve with all that? The deli, sushi, pizza, any kind of sandwich. Salads. Perfect for a guy who doesn't cook."

She looked where he pointed, and it made him wonder if she liked cooking. "Of course, if somebody wants to cook for me, I'm down with that. Do you cook?"

"Of course I do. Remember, I was raised on a commune. We grew our own stuff, slaughtered our own meat." That made her pause—it wasn't something she liked to remember, even if it was part of her past. "Yeah, but my cooking is much more refined these days."

"Hang on. You butchered your own food?"

She nodded and hesitated before answering, because most people didn't understand. "Yes, I did. I grew up with it, so it was normal. But, as I grew older, I appreciated the animals and their sacrifice."

"Even though I'm in the cattle industry, it still bothers me. We follow Temple Grandin's principles for the health and well-being of the animal. Anyway, let's put all this aside and do some shopping."

"Sounds good. Anything in particular you like?"

"Everything. Oh, except Brussels sprouts."

For some reason Jimi thought that inordinately funny and burst out laughing. "Of all things! Brussels sprouts."

Dallas curled his lip and said, "My mom would make them. Boiled. Even the smell turns my stomach."

"I see. I think you just challenged me."

Dallas led her around the store, and Jimi was blown away by the whole ambience of it. The lighting, the signage, the flow of the displays. It made shopping enjoyable. Normally she'd fly into a store, grab what she needed and get the hell out. But this store made her want to wander around, discover each new display or basket full of some kind of treat. "I love being in this store. It makes me feel good."

He raised a brow. "A grocery store makes you feel good?"

She smiled and nodded, lifting a pineapple she sniffed for ripeness before putting it in the buggy he was pushing around. "Yes, it does. It turns me on."

His eyebrows shot up. "Seriously, as in sexual? That's the strangest thing I've ever heard."

"Not so strange, really. I know a few women who feel the same."

"That's just plain weird." He shook his head. "How the hell are you ever supposed to understand women?" He drove the buggy over to a big fruit display. She followed.

"Maybe you're not," she offered.

"Do you like papaya?" he asked and reached for one.

"I love all fruit. We can't get it this fresh and delicious looking back home."

"I've called it 'pawpaw' since I was a kid." He picked one up. "This one looks good. Great with some good cheese, sliced Italian sausage and some fine red wine. We'll get some of that, too." He handed it to her.

Jimi sniffed it before putting it in the buggy.

"Why do you smell it?" he asked.

She shrugged her shoulders. "My dad taught me. He said you can smell the ripeness, so I smell it. Something I never really gave thought to until you pointed it out. But he's right."

Dallas picked up the pineapple and smelled it. "I can smell the sweetness of it. Hmm, who knew—never really paid attention to it before, either."

They wandered off side by side, selecting groceries. It gave her an image of what the future could be like with him. Domesticated. Family. Fun. He reached for tomatoes, his muscles bulging and rippling by the simple move, and it got her heart all fluttery. He glanced at her, his eyes expressive. She saw his passion simmering. Waiting to be unleashed.

It would be intense, too. His underlying sensuality kept her in a smoldering state of arousal. Would that subside over time? She was beginning to wonder if they had some kind of special connection. Having met under dire circumstances. Could a relationship grow from that? Their banter back and forth was effortless. She didn't feel uncomfortable with him; nor did he seem so with her. It seemed natural. Right. New and very unfamiliar feelings began to take root inside her and frightened her a little bit, but also gave her the strangest sensation of hope.

They wandered in comfortable silence. Through the produce section into the bakery area, where Jimi's mouth started to water at the sights and smells at the cornucopia of all sorts of breads and bakery treats.

Carbs. Her downfall. She could pass on the chocolate, cake and candies, but put a bag of chips or plate of fries in front of her and she was weak. She touched a loaf snugly wrapped in a paper wrapper and sighed with delight at the softness under her fingers.

She wanted to take everything because it looked so delicious. What would the next few days bring? She had the time, just not any necessities with her. How long would she stay with him? She knew at least one night. Her heart fluttered thinking of what was to come later.

"Smell that bread. What is it about the fresh-baked aroma that is just so homey and makes you want to buy everything?" Dallas said, and held a big breath after he said that.

"I know. There's nothing like the smell of fresh bread. It's been so long since I've made it."

"Seriously? You've made bread, too?"

Jimi was tickled by the look of surprise on his face. "Yes. I've made bread. Remember I grew up—"

"Yes, and yes. I know where you grew up. So maybe you can make some for me?"

"Maybe. It's a long process to make bread."

They both fell silent, looking at each other. She wondered if he was thinking the same as her. How long would they be together? Would there be time to bake bread?

"Let's grab a couple of loaves and get on out of here. Sound good?"

"Yes." Jimi smiled and stood up on her toes to give him a kiss on the cheek. An impulsive move to be sure, here in the store, but the urge was too powerful to ignore.

The touch of his skin next to her lips was polarizing. Jimi drew in a sharp breath at her reaction. Dallas also appeared to hold his breath, and when he turned to face her, she was caught in his gaze. There was so much emotion in his eyes it gave her a lump in her throat.

This man certainly had some kind of power over her.

His lips were so close she couldn't resist. There, in the middle of the store, they kissed. His hands held her hips steady as she leaned into him. The world around them faded away and it was only them. No one else. Among the organic produce and next to the artisan breads, Jimi felt the first pull of…dare she say it? *Love.* With tomatoes on one side, pineapples on the other, and shoppers pushing their carts around them, she allowed herself to get lost in his embrace. She knew she'd never look at grocery shopping the same way. Ever again.

Maybe dreams do come true in blue Hawaii.

Breathless, she reluctantly pulled away from him. "This really isn't the place to be making out."

He nodded and stepped back, passion and something else etched on his face. "You might be right."

Jimi furrowed her brows, not really understanding the look she'd seen flash across his face. "Is something wrong?"

Now she felt a little unnerved that he seemed to be holding back. Did he not want to be seen with her? Maybe he wasn't good at PDA. She forced herself not to jump to any conclusions.

Live in the moment, girl.

"Nothing. I agree with you. Not the right place to be getting all hot under the collar." He smiled. "How about we pay for the groceries and head over to the other store so you can get some clothes and then be on our way?"

"Ooh, clothes shopping. Do you really know what you're in for?"

Dallas laughed. "Likely not."

JIMI LOVED THIS STORE. The bright, happy atmosphere fit so well with Hawaii culture and the vacation mood. It was a visual rainbow of brightly colored beachwear.

"Do you have a pool at your place?" Whatever he bought for her today, she had every intention of reimbursing him. And she was liking the look of the bathing suits. "I'll let you buy me these clothes under one condition. That I pay you back and you don't argue about it. Otherwise, I can't come with you." She stared at him and held her breath, not wanting him to argue back. He didn't, so she continued with her negotiation. She had no idea what he could afford and didn't want to overstep. "Can you give me an idea on budget?"

He smiled, not giving any sign he took offense. "Get whatever you like, and we'll sort it out later."

She was relieved. Not knowing his income level and salary range for ranch workers was beyond her scope of knowledge.

She nodded, accepting his offer gracefully. "I am paying you back! No argument about that."

"Like I said," Dallas answered, "we'll worry about it all later. For now, it's fun time. Grab some stuff that you need for a couple of days and we'll take it all in stride."

A couple of *days*? Heat rushed through her body in

anticipation of spending the next few days with him. Alone. And not in a damp and rainy mountainside camp.

"These are so pretty." She held up a pareo, the colors vibrant and beautiful shades of tangerine. "Are they made on the island?"

Dallas lifted the edge where the tag was. "Yep, made on island."

Jimi felt stupid. Why hadn't she thought to look at the tag? Of course it would say where it was made. She would know that, being in the fashion industry. She selected a couple of them, the beautiful tangerine, and a hot-pink-and-purple one. She didn't have a bathing suit and justified it that you could never have too many bikinis. She looked for one that would match both of her sarongs. She held one up.

"Do you like this?"

"I love an itsy-bitsy teeny-weeny bikini. Even if it's not yellow polka dots."

Jimi laughed and handed it to him to hold. "You're very patient."

"I have a sister—what can I say."

Jimi smiled. "Larson, right?" She recalled the other guests had mentioned she and Dallas were siblings. "She's a ranch hand, too?"

He nodded and watched in silence as Jimi shoved some hangers aside until she found a couple of colorful tank tops in her size. He took them from her and laid them across his arm. "My brother, Tucker, is as well, when he's not off doing stupid shit or flitting in and out of his shop."

"Yes, I remember Tucker. A family affair."

"That it is."

"You know, that's really nice. A family all together, doing something they love. You all do love it, right?"

"Oh yes, we love it. Our family has been ranching for over one-hundred-and-fifty years."

"That's really something. I would have never guessed it on Hawaii."

"It sure is. There are a couple of ranching families on the island. What about your family?"

Jimi focused on the shorts, fingering through the sizes. "Well, you know I grew up on a commune."

He nodded. "I find that fascinating. I'd like to hear about it sometime."

She looked at him. "Most people do." Relieved she didn't have to get into it here, she selected a pair of white-and-black shorts. "Sure, when I'm liquored up enough."

He chuckled. "That bad, huh?"

She smiled at him and lifted a shoulder. "Interesting enough, put it that way." Wandering to the next rack, she exclaimed, "Ooh, look at this."

Jimi held up a lovely long-sleeved ivory cover-up. It was so light and filmy, delicately woven, that it looked like spun silk. Filigree threads, soft and silky, with loose loopy stitches and a slightly tapered shape. She held it out and decided she had to have it.

"I love this store." She looked around with an assessing eye and realized there was a lot she could do with it. The tropical theme was lovely, with some unique items, but it could use an infusion of a few higher-end products to complement the island theme. Like her clothing line. Excitement bloomed in her chest as an idea began to form.

"You do? Well, I'm glad I brought you here, then."

"Me, too."

She needed panties and spied some at the far end of the store, where a selection of very pretty undergarments was displayed. Jimi was in heaven.

"I'd like you to pick for me," she told Dallas with a mischievous grin.

He looked at the neatly arranged array of rainbow-colored underthings. "Me? You want me to choose this stuff?"

"Why not? I'm curious to see what you like. A man's perspective."

"Hmm, okay. Let's see…" He gave all of his attention to selecting four pairs of the prettiest panties she'd ever seen.

"I see you like the minimalistic look."

"I can already imagine how they're going to look on you."

"Mmm, well, okay then. This is getting more and more interesting." Jimi was wound up pretty tight with the anticipation of spending some naked time with him. Now the urge to get the shopping over with was paramount.

She decided she didn't need bras since she had the bikini top. Plus, she was lucky enough to have stand-up boobies, so she could go without one if it came down to it. The girls could go free for the next few days. Desire rushed through her and she felt her nipples harden. Yes, it was definitely time to get out of here and alone with this amazing man.

12

THANKFUL FOR THE rush of island air that came in the open window to cool the flush that still warmed her body, Jimi watched the scenery and the varied landscapes. The drive wasn't too long and she was enchanted by the island. Even more so when they drove into a lush and tropical location. She wondered if his house was close now.

"Wow, it's so beautiful." Jimi was like a bobblehead, trying to take in all the scenery.

"I know. I never get tired of it."

"It's so different on this side of the island."

"It is. There are eight climate zones or eleven to thirteen, depending on who you talk to, from humid tropical to arid to tundra. Where we're going is very lush, tropical and not like you saw when you were biking."

Jimi laughed. "What do you mean about the climate zones?"

"It can be sunny and hot in Kona and gale force winds by Hawi." Dallas smiled and then turned back to the road.

"I wasn't really expecting the arid, almost desert-looking area. I expected to see palm trees and flowers and waterfalls everywhere. This island seems so much more rugged. Mmm, just smell that wonderful air."

"You don't like air-conditioning?"

"Only when I'm sleeping *if* it's hot, but I prefer the fresh air. I love an open window so I can smell the breeze and feel it on my body. Hearing the night sounds and waking to the birds is heaven. I guess that comes from my childhood."

They fell silent for a moment.

"So what did you think of the wedding, the camping expedition?" Dallas asked her.

"It was interesting. I hadn't roughed it like that since I was a kid. I must say I got out of the habit of being down-to-earth and had gotten way too used to being pampered. It brought me back to reality in a hurry."

She liked that he smiled when she said that.

"Now, it's hard to imagine you as a pampered princess."

"Not so hard, really. I was one, at least as a grown-up. Not as a child. I certainly didn't look the part when I arrived at the ranch, though." She remembered how frazzled, ragged and lost she'd been getting off the bus. So out of sorts at all the things that had gone wrong. "Not having my own clothes and all my paraphernalia, and depending on the generosity of others certainly was humbling."

"I wasn't complaining. I like your *earthy* appeal."

That struck her as outrageously funny and Jimi burst out laughing. "*Earthy!* That's probably the nicest thing anyone has ever said about me. I've never thought of myself as earthy, but you know what? I like it."

She stared at him, thinking. Earthy. For the first time in her life she actually didn't mind someone knowing about her commune upbringing. Unknowingly, he'd helped her see past the stigma. She'd definitely been earthy as a child, and now she could see how far she'd tried to run from it, hiding behind clothes and makeup, only to come around full circle back to the basics.

The look he cast her was smolderingly hot, and she swallowed at the burst of erotic heat that boiled through her blood, making her heart beat a little bit faster. It was surprising how easy it was being with him. No pretenses, airs, the need to be runway ready, even though she *wasn't* a model. She could just *be* with him and that was so wonderfully liberating. She felt devilishly sexy around him, too. Jimi drew in a big, contented sigh and gazed out the window, quite happy with the direction this little side trip was taking.

"Why do you like earthy?" Her curiosity needed an answer.

He shrugged. "I don't know. I guess because I am. Just a simple kind of guy who enjoys the simple things in life. It fits with me."

"Mmm-hmm," she mused. That really got her thinking about all sorts of things. Jimi sensed she was barreling down a road that was going to have a fork in it. And she'd have to choose which way to go.

"Look to your left. You'll be able to catch a glimpse of the ocean through the trees. We'll be coming up to the turn soon that will take us down to my house."

Excitement brewed in her at the immediacy of their interlude fast approaching. She looked where he indicated and gasped when the beauty of the ocean flickered through the trees. She was eager to see what his house looked like, and then the reality of it all set in. She was in a strange place, with a strange—sort of—man, and no one knew where she was. She swallowed nervously. Okay, she admitted to herself, as much as this tryst promised to be exciting, it was suddenly a little bit nerve-racking.

Was it too late to change her mind? *It's never too late.* But did she want to change her mind and go back to her hotel? Alone.

No.

Anxiously she watched the road ahead, realizing she had no clue what kind of place he lived in. She had no preconceived notion of his lifestyle, other than he was a ranch hand. The truck was clearly a farm truck, so she wondered at his status, as well. How much money did a ranch hand make? Then she felt guilty for even wondering about it. It wasn't any of her business and not what was important, either. It was the man who was important. And everything about him had shown her the kind of man he was. Otherwise, she wouldn't be with him. There, she'd settled her nerves.

Watching Dallas from behind her windblown hair, she knew she liked him. A lot. So, she would just let the chips fall where they may. It was still too fresh, new, to even think about a future together. And the fact that she even let that thought creep into her mind—more than once—made her ponder the future. Could she live here? As much as she liked the beauty of it, her business was across the continent. Almost a thirteen-hour flight away. Too far for a long-distance relationship. She shoved the thought from her mind and decided not to dwell on it.

Dallas turned off and drove along a laneway, through a green tunnel of arching tree branches, towering palms and flowers clinging to the foliage.

"Oh, my God. Are those orchids?"

"Yes, they are. And there's a lot more flowers around here."

"I love flowers."

"Most women do."

"I can't get over how beautiful this is, doesn't matter how many times I have to say it." Jimi leaned her head out the car window, inhaling the wonderful scent and loving how her hair streamed out behind her. Sunlight dappled across the ground and Jimi drew in a breath when a house appeared around the next bend.

"Oh my, it's so beautiful. Wasn't it damaged by the hurricane?" she asked him.

"Whenever I'm not here, I lower the hurricane shields on the windows. So far I've been fortunate nothing too drastic has happened. Just a few branches to clear away."

"I'm blown away by your house."

"Why? What did you expect?"

He pulled up in front of the wide slab steps that led to a beautiful porch. The house, made of wood and a black rough stone, held a very Hawaiian appeal. Flowers were everywhere at the front of the house.

"I honestly had no idea. But not this! It's spectacular."

Dallas came around and opened her truck door, helping her down. He reached into the back and grabbed all the bags.

"Here, let me help." Jimi took what she could manage while he easily carried the rest, shaking out his keys to unlock the heavy front door. She could see through the beveled glass a teasing glimpse into his house and couldn't wait until the door was open for her to see it properly.

"Oh, wow. This is amazing."

Dallas let her enter before him and it took her breath away. Even with the windows shuttered, she could tell how lovely the house was.

"Over to the right is the kitchen."

After putting the bags on the counter, she watched Dallas open all the storm blinds to reveal the view beyond. It was even more stunning with the sun streaming in. She followed him through the wide living area out to the sweeping deck after he'd pushed the glass walls to the side, tucking them into their secret hiding compartments on either side of the room.

"Come." He took her hand and she curled her fingers around his. This man was full of surprises and wiggling his way even more into her heart. They stepped onto the deck and she dragged her gaze away from him to see where he'd taken her. The deck ran the width of the house, with a Plexiglas front so as not to obscure the magnificent view.

"Oh, Dallas. Look." They were perched on top of a cliff with an unbelievable vista that seemed to drop away to the sea below. Craggy black outcrops ringed them, covered in lush trees, bushes and flowers. "This is simply amazing."

"I have to agree."

She felt him come up behind her, placing his hands on the railing and pinning her between his powerful arms and rock-hard chest. She was becoming addicted to his touch.

"I don't want to be anywhere except here. With you," she whispered, closing her eyes. Jimi lifted her face, enjoying the breeze coming in from the ocean. He sighed and they stood that way for a little while. Quiet. Content. But she wasn't immune to the energy radiating from him, wrapping her in its sultry embrace. The rustle of the trees and palm fronds serenaded them. "I love that sound and could get used to hearing it morning, noon and night." She kept her voice as a whisper, not wanting to drown out any nature sounds. "I could get used to this."

"Get used to what?"

Jimi opened her eyes and waved her hand in front of her. "Being here with you like this. Everything. I love it. As much as I hate to admit it, it reminds me of how we kids were raised. Maybe I'm only now appreciating the country way of life and the simplicity, even with its complications. If that makes any sense." She returned her gaze to the vista in front of them. "Is there a way down?"

"Yes, there are some steps, but they are very steep and tricky."

Jimi clutched the railing and leaned over to look below. His arms squeezed on her sides.

"Careful now. I don't want you to go tumbling over."

She liked how he cared. It was a new feeling to have someone actually give a shit about her. The craggy black rock and the crashing surf below was beautiful. It seemed so raw and angry, and yet a breathtaking sight.

"I'd like to go down. Is there a beach?"

"There is a small cove, only accessible at low tide."

"That sounds almost magical."

"It is." He pushed back from her and Jimi immediately missed his presence. "Make yourself at home. I'm going to unpack the groceries."

"I can help you do that."

She took his hand and they walked back into the house.

"Your house is lovely. Did you build it?"

"No, it's been here for a while. My parents owned it first, and then I bought it from them. Did some updating."

"Why didn't they want to live here anymore?"

He was silent and she turned to look at him. Had she said something wrong?

"My mom just didn't want to live here anymore." He paused and Jimi wondered if she'd touched on a sensitive topic. "So what can I get you to drink? Some of the wine we bought today? Or I make a mean mai tai. I may not know my way around the kitchen, but I do know my way around a bar."

"I'd love a mean mai tai." She was dying to ask him why his mother wouldn't want to live in a place like this, but she felt the timing wasn't right. Obviously, he didn't want to talk about his parents. Fine. She wasn't going to pry and would respect his privacy as she would like hers respected.

"Feel free to wander around while I make the drinks."

"I will, thanks." In an impulsive move, Jimi hugged him, wrapping her arms around his neck. She thrilled when he caught her in a big bear hug and swung her around. "I'm so glad you brought me here." She giggled and, when he let her go, she lingered in his embrace for a few seconds.

"I'm glad you came."

With a skip in her step and a heart full of happy, Jimi wandered back into the living area and through a door to a hall on the other side of the room. She paused, glancing over her shoulder, and smiled when he met her gaze.

I haven't felt this happy in...forever.

Following the hallway, she looked out the windows to her left, seeing the driveway they'd just driven up. The wide, brightly lit hall ran the length of the house. It wasn't a huge house. It was a nice size, and she dared to think of her waking up here every morning. *With him.* A shiver of delight ran through her. Yes, she could imagine the mornings, waking up in Dallas's warm, comforting embrace.

Three doors lined the hall on the right, the first a cute bedroom that had an inner door to a really nice bathroom with a wonderfully deep tub and a view the same as the living room. Farther down was a very well-equipped office with a huge old desk that looked as if it was carved from one chunk of wood.

"I wonder if it's made from island wood," Jimi mused.

She eyed the closed door at the end of the hall. Her heart thumped a little harder.

"I bet that's the master bedroom." She crept up to the door, almost feeling like an intruder. She placed her hands on the knob. Taking a breath, she hesitated for a second before turning and gently pushing it open.

"Oh, my God."

It was a master bedroom and absolutely stunning. It seemed to jut out over the cliff, as if it were suspended, and three walls were all glass. A king-size bed was positioned just before the window and it was a few steps up. The deck wrapped all the way around to here. A hot tub, too! She could imagine sitting in the tub with wine, watching the stars.

"Just wow. I can totally imagine myself waking up in that bed tomorrow morning." Jimi hugged herself at the thrill of excitement that rippled through her body. Not so much about the house but because of Dallas.

The decor was very tropical, with honey-colored wood, a vaulted ceiling and light-colored floors. The furniture was very Hawaiian, as were the closet doors. Vibrant pillows with a matching duvet cover draped on the bed. Jimi was impressed. She spied another door on the far side of the room. Could it get any better?

"Yes!"

An en suite that rivaled the one at her hotel. In fact, this one was even better. She felt she'd just stepped into a tropical jungle, all clear glass windows looking into the rain forest. No view of the cliffs and ocean, but the soft greens and dappled sunlight, ferns and flowers in every color of the rainbow painted a picture Monet couldn't have mastered and filled the panorama just outside the glass.

"Wow," she whispered when she saw the shower.

It was doorless, big and tiled shoulder high, where glass then replaced the remaining height. She walked over and stepped inside, twirling around and looking up. An array of showerheads lined the ceiling, just like the walls. She was determined to get him into this shower tomorrow morning, and she knew that was going to happen because she was just as determined to be sleeping here, in his arms and bed. Tonight.

Jimi was so enthralled by this room that when Dallas slipped his hands around her waist from behind she nearly jumped out of her skin.

"Oh, you scared the hell out of me!"

"Sorry." He nuzzled her neck and Jimi sighed.

"You have a wonderful home."

"I'm glad you like it."

"Mmm-hmm. I do."

She leaned back against his powerful chest, his muscles hard like granite next to her. He splayed his fingers over her belly, pressing with an almost possessive grip, which she liked very much. His hand inched lower, his fingertip slipping under the waistband of her shorts while the other slid up to cup her breast.

"Oh, Dallas." The words fell softly from her lips as she got lost in the sensation.

Resting her head on his shoulder, she closed her eyes so she could focus on his touch. With him behind her, and the way his hands searched along her flesh, she was spellbound. Aroused. For him.

"I love how you feel," Dallas whispered into her ear, his breath rustling her hair.

"I love how you touch me." Jimi murmured the words on a breathy moan.

She sucked in a gasp when his fingers slipped beneath her shorts. Exploring lower while at the same time his mouth found the curve of her neck, pressing delicious little kisses until he found her earlobe.

"I haven't showered."

"I don't care, and if it bothers you that much... Where are we?"

Jimi opened her eyes and smiled.

"I guess we can fix that right here."

"And so much better than the chilly rain shower up at the camp."

She moaned and moistened her lips when his fingers slid a little farther until he found her clit. Jimi drew in a sharp breath and she reached behind to grasp his hips. Clutching him, she pushed her butt back and loved the feel of his cock pressing into her. He made a sound so deep it sounded like a growl. It thrilled her she was able to excite him as much as he did her.

She wiggled her hips into his cock as his fingers pressed deeper into her folds.

"You're wet."

"I—I know."

"And trembling."

She nodded in agreement, unable to form words as his fingers played with her.

"I like that."

"O-ohh, your talking i-is… Mmm." Words escaped her when he pressed lower and the heel of his hand put delicious pressure on her clit. Letting go of his hips, she tried to shove down her bike shorts, but they caught around her knees.

Dallas spun her around until she faced him.

He was gazing at her with his ever expressive and now half-closed eyes, passion boiling in their depths. It ran deep and powerful, stealing her breath away. Could he be feeling the same powerful connection as she was?

"You know, I've never really seen you properly naked. Maybe it's about time. Arms up."

She did as she was told.

He pulled off her top and then reached behind her, all the while keeping his eyes locked on hers as he expertly flicked open the snaps on her bra before removing and tossing it outside the shower. Her shorts were still tangled around her knees and she was unable to move, fearing she'd trip and collapse at his feet. Then, before she could process it, he was on his knees in front of her, tugging her shorts down. His hands, so gentle on her feet, lifted them one at a time, and then her shorts joined her bra on the floor.

"Oh!" she exclaimed when he pressed his face to her belly and his hands grasped her ass. His fingers dug into her skin and yanked her closer. She didn't resist, loving how he took command. It was exciting. New. And she welcomed it, glad for the strength of his grip. *Oh, Lord*, she thought as his tongue swirled in her belly button, gently pulling on her belly button jewel. Shots of liquid desire seared a path down to her core. Every nerve in her body lit up under his touch. She was in excruciating ecstasy.

"Shower," she whispered, knowing where he was headed and feeling the desperate urge to wash the sheen of dry perspiration from her body. Jimi thrust her fingers into his hair just as his lips found the top of her cleft and his tongue prodded just as his mouth closed on her. She looked down at him, and he was looking up, his lips tight to her body. She pulled his head until he tipped his head back. The passion glazing his eyes told her he didn't care in the least for her concern.

She released his hair and let her head fall back to the tiles when his mouth found her pussy. She stumbled as the explosive touch of his tongue sweeping through her hypersensitive flesh made her legs give way. She was close to mindless when she reached for the side knob, turning it until a burst of water from the ceiling showered over them. They both let out a shout when the cool water hit their heated skin. Quickly she twisted the knob and sighed when warm water streamed over them.

Dallas held her firm, helping her back up until she rested on the wall.

"Sit down." His voice was muffled.

She let him lower her to the wooden seat, his mouth never lifting from her. She was putty in his hands. He raised her leg and rested her ankle on his shoulder. A shiver rippled along her skin as he caressed his way up to her hip, squeezing her flesh. With one shoulder still holding her leg wide, Dallas leaned back and gazed at her, fully exposed to him.

"Oh, my." Jimi closed her eyes, and rested her head back on the wall.

It was one of the most erotic things she'd ever experienced. Her trembling increased and her teeth chattered. Not from cold, but from the intensity of the expression she'd seen on his face.

"You are beautiful."

She opened her eyes, not wanting to miss a thing. Water streamed over them. His hair was now wet and curled at the ends, and his lips glistened, shiny from the water…and from her. She drew in a breath, raising her chest when his free hand reached and found her breast. She watched him touch her and drew in a shaky breath when he rubbed his thumb across her nipple, moaning when she saw the way it rose in response to his stroking.

Jimi reached for him when Dallas took the rigid peak between his lips, suckling on her and flicking his tongue over the supersensitive flesh, then moving lower, finding her clitoris. The sensation of his lips, tongue and the rain shower beating down on her was almost sensation overload.

Jimi was unable to control the trembling that rushed over her body as his tongue continued to explore her. Moving lower again, where she truly wanted him. The featherlight touch of his fingers along her side raised goose bumps in its wake, until his hand rested in the crease of her thigh. Right alongside his mouth.

"Ooh, Dallas," she uttered when his fingers swirled around her opening as his lips and tongue worked magic on her clit.

He pressed into her, laved at her with his tongue, driving her into a frenzy of twitching muscles as her orgasm built in her belly. She thrust her hands into his hair, fearing she might fall off the earth if she didn't hang on to him. He must have sensed her climax was near and expertly teased her body closer.

She moaned, and the spray of the shower running over them only intensified the wildly erotic sensations. Surely the heat from her body would turn the water into steam, just as the hot lava did as it reached the ocean after boiling out of the volcano. In a hissing, blistering frenzy.

That was her, a volcano of molten lava waiting to blow into an explosive and glorious eruption of exquisite delight.

Her orgasm bore down on her, but she didn't want it to come just yet. She wanted to enjoy what he was doing to her as long as possible. He was wonderfully talented and knew exactly where to touch. When to curl his fingers just so. The time to flick his tongue and where, when to pause to drive her to dizzying heights. When he did pause, she looked down at him.

He glanced up at her from between her thighs, not stopping with his insanely fabulous attention to her. He stared at her and she back at him. Watching him. It made her feel like a bad girl, in a good and naughty way, to watch as he licked her, the way his fingers slipped in and out of her and how his eyelids fluttered the more she moaned and cried out with delight.

She shook her head and tried to talk, but all she could mumble was "N-n-no…d-don't stop." She met his gaze again. "K-keep going. So…so close…"

She'd never been so thoroughly loved by a man's mouth before and she didn't want it to stop. Ever. Not even when her orgasm swept over her and he had to hold her tight as her muscles overtook her body, contracting and pulsing in the most mind-blowing way. She let out a cry that echoed from the vaulted ceiling and gripped his hair so tight it had to hurt him. But he didn't let up. Not until her body finally calmed down and ceased its orgasmic tremors.

Jimi drew in a deep breath and let it out long and slow. "Aah, D-Dallas, what have you done to me?"

"Love you, *hemahema*. Just loved you."

She smiled and brushed the hair from his brow. He stood, taking fragrant shower gel, rubbing it over her body then swiftly washing the suds away before wrapping her in a towel. She was in heaven and let him take care of her, suddenly exhausted and sated.

Once she was cocooned in a soft towel, Dallas carried her to the bed. The sun was beginning to set when he placed her under the covers.

"Ho'onanea."

"What's that mean?" Jimi asked.

"Relax." He joined her on the bed after shucking off his wet clothes, and pulled her into his embrace. "Let's watch the sun go down."

"So much has happened since our first sunset. I can't even remember how many days ago it was now."

"I know. I'm glad you're here."

She snuggled into him. "Me, too."

13

"Is THERE A table on the deck?" Jimi asked.

"Yes. Here, let me take something." Dallas reached for the tray.

"What about the mai tais from earlier? We never drank them." Jimi asked, "Would you mind getting them? Pretty please."

How could he resist her cheeky smile? "Sure, but I could always make us fresh ones. We hadn't planned on snoozing after the sun set."

"I know, but I don't want to waste the drinks. All they need is a bit of ice."

Jimi put down the tray of food and he reached out, curling his arm around her waist.

"C'mere, you," he growled. She gave a sexy little gasp of surprise and twirled into him. She flattened her palms against his bare chest. Her touch was electric, and he drew in a sharp breath at the heat sizzling between them. Tightening his grip on her waist, he ran a hand up her back and into the hair at the nape of her neck, cradling her head.

"Oh, Dallas. What's happening with us?"

He stared down into her eyes, pondering the question she'd just asked him. He shook his head, not really sure what was going on, himself. "All I know is I like spending time with you. Getting to know you."

He'd been concerned about starting something up with her at the camp. But it had happened and led him here. Maybe worrying about it had been wrong. Avoiding hookups with guests had been easy. Until Jimi. And thinking of this as a hookup completely offended him now. This was beginning to be anything *but* a hookup. There was more going on here and he was being drawn in deeper and deeper, enough that he had to see where it was all going. Even if it meant she would leave in the end. His feelings were growing and he owed it to himself, and her, to discover just how deep. Even if it was opening up a Pandora's box for them. One or both of them could get hurt.

She nodded and licked her lips. His eyes dropped to her mouth and watched as she moistened them. "I know. This is so surprising. And so powerful. I—I don't know what to think, except spending time with you is the only thing I want to do."

"Then we'd best make the most of our time." He grabbed her in a frantic hug, pulling her tight as if she might be all a wonderful dream and he was going to wake up any moment.

"Yes, we'd best."

Jimi wrapped her arms around his neck, her flesh so

warm next to him and it sent a bolt of desire through him. *No, this is not a dream.* Nor was it just sex with her, which was fantastic, obviously. It was everything about her. He couldn't even begin to itemize the *everything*, either. All he knew was he needed to taste her again. Crushing his mouth onto hers felt like he was coming home. He reached out with his tongue, and when hers met his, he felt it right down into his balls. He grew hard and thrust his hips toward her, loving how she moaned into his mouth. Her hands pulling on his hair only escalated his desire.

He kissed her until they were breathless. His world seem to tip and Dallas spread his legs to support them. She clung to him, and he loved how that felt. Like she needed him and wanted to get inside him. Everything that he wanted, too. He let himself drown in the sweetness of her kiss, knowing she was here only for a finite time. It almost gave him a sense of panic mixed in with his ramping arousal.

"How long you here for?" he asked when he lifted his lips from hers. Her eyes were closed, her cheeks flushed, and all he wanted to do was carry her off to bed and make love to her.

"Mmm, oh…" Her voice was breathless and she had a hard time thinking straight. Dallas smiled, knowing he'd done that to her. "Th-three weeks. But close to a week gone already, so two? I can't think straight. Don't make me think. I just want to feel, be with you right now."

"So that means I have two weeks with you? Before you have to go home." That thought utterly devastated him and his chest tightened. Either he was in the blush of infatuation or something more was happening here.

She nodded. "And it's going to go by so fast. Please don't remind me," she whispered.

Were those tears sparkling in her eyes? If Dallas didn't know better, he'd say she was about to cry. His heart swelled with emotion. He drew her into a tight hug and rested his chin on the top of her head.

"Then we'll savor every second." She nodded and tightened her arms around him. He was surprised as hell when he felt the hot sting of tears in his own eyes. He couldn't remember the last time something had moved him so. It unnerved him a little bit that she was able to invoke such powerful emotions in him. Dallas kissed the top of her head and disentangled himself from her. "Now, how about we start savoring those moments right now. Let me go and get those mai tais."

Dallas couldn't be more confused about everything going on right now. In one second he was never wanting her to leave, and then, on the heels of that, he was scared shitless by how much this woman made him feel.

Taking a breather, and getting himself back together in the bedroom, were a few moments that he needed to try to sort things out. But he didn't do that great a job when he saw the rumpled bedsheets reminding how nicely she fit next to him. He drew in a deep sigh. One positive thing—she was no longer a client, a guest at the ranch. So that released him from that sense of duty. She was just a woman he was strongly attracted to in every way possible. He knew he was opening himself up for pain. To be hurt again. Could their lives together ever work?

"So, man up and let's see where this takes us," he told the quiet room. Dallas grabbed the two drinks and wandered back down the hall, through the living room to find her relaxed on a lounge, looking up at the stars.

"This is so incredible." Jimi pointed up at the sky. "I don't think I've ever seen such amazing stars."

Dallas put the drinks down on the table between them and stretched out on the other lounge. He crossed his feet and laced his fingers together behind his head to stare up at the sky. "Yes, it is. I never get tired of stargazing. Did you know we have astronomical observatories on Maunakea?"

"No, I didn't. Why Hawaii? It doesn't seem like it is as high an elevation as other places in the world."

"From my understanding, it's because the atmosphere is extremely dry and cloud free. Plus, it's still a pretty high elevation." He was glad of this conversation, which steered them away from his earlier feelings. He felt like he needed a little more time to process things.

"Wow, that's so interesting. Have you ever been up there?"

"A long time ago—they have a visitor station now and lots of rules."

"Humph. Seems to be the way of things now, doesn't it. Rules. I need to start breaking some rules."

Dallas laughed. "Why am I not surprised by that?"

"What do you mean?" She was laughing, too, and he enjoyed their playful banter.

"Just that it's never boring with you. I like that."

"That's a good thing," she teased. "I'd hate to be boring and predictable."

"I highly doubt you could be, even if you tried."

"I'm going to take that as something you like *and* as a compliment." She stood and picked up the plate of food. "Here, I bet you're hungry. I know I am."

"Looks great. Thanks." He grabbed some cheese and a pineapple spear and popped both into his mouth. "This is the best combination." Dallas munched, liking the explosion of flavor.

She picked a piece of pineapple and sucked on it. All he could think of was those lips wrapped around his cock doing the same thing. Dallas grabbed the drink and chugged it down.

WHAT A DAY. A glorious one. This morning's cycling travesty seemed like ages ago. Not the same day as today. So much great stuff had happened since then it was almost mind-boggling. Jimi turned to look at Dallas lounging back on the chair. How this man had come into her life and in such a freight-train sort of way was also mind-boggling. This whole trip to Hawaii was so out of the ordinary it was fantastic. It was what she'd needed to pull her out of the doldrums of her life. And she wasn't even thinking of her business back home. That in itself was extremely shocking. Could she ever let go of the life she'd so carefully created?

"You know, the living-each-day-as-it-comes style isn't too bad. But I have a business back home that needs me. I'm trying not to think about it all right now." She sighed and sucked on a spear of pineapple. Dallas turned and looked at her, smiling and not saying anything. Which was okay. She liked that about him, that they could have comfortable silence. It didn't seem like they had to fill any void with *stuff*. Plus, he could kiss her senseless, which was a big bonus.

And something she never figured she would experience.

"Isn't that the nature of the game? Living in the moment." She could never get tired of hearing his voice.

Jimi nodded and sucked the juice off her fingers. "Something that the past few days has certainly made me understand. It wasn't something that had ever entered my mind before."

"You're aiming for some trouble if you keep doing that." His low and sexy voice draped around her like hot honey and Jimi paused, finger in her mouth, to look at him.

She raised her eyebrows and asked with feigned innocence, "What do you mean? What am I doing that is going to get me in trouble?"

"Sucking on your fingers."

Fingers still in her mouth, Jimi smiled and decided a little bit of teasing would do him some good. So she swirled her tongue around the fingertip, and his eyes widened. He shifted on the lounge chair and she dropped her gaze past his magnificently muscled chest down to the waistband of his shorts. "Oh my, I see something is happening." She giggled and grabbed another piece of pineapple.

"What do you expect? He has a mind of his own, especially when a sexy woman like you is sucking on fingers when you should really be sucking on something else."

Jimi threw back her head and laughed out loud. "Is that right? And just what should this woman be sucking on?"

"You're a smart girl. I'm sure you can figure it out."

"Yes, I am a smart girl." She smiled and prowled over to him, liking how he fidgeted on the lounge. She playfully slapped his hand away when he reached up and took hold of the edge of the sarong she'd wrapped around herself earlier. "No touchy until I say."

Dallas dropped his hand and lay back. He looked as if he was about to explode out of his skin. The bulge in his shorts so tantalizingly tempting, Jimi was eager to get them off him. The juice of the pineapple drifted around her fingers and she held her hand over his chest. Jimi squeezed the fruit until a stream of juice dripped onto his chest, pooling in between the muscles of his pecs.

He hissed but remained still as a statue.

Jimi leaned down, the urge to lick him overpowering. His chest rose and fell with his deep breathing, making the juice spill over and trickle down lower. Across his stomach, running in rivulets between the ridges of his muscled belly and pooling in his belly button. She squeezed the pineapple, and more juice slicked over his belly, darkening the line of hair that disappeared beneath his shorts.

"Off, shorts…" Jimi's tongue was tied at the sight of him before her. Sexy, muscled, aroused. He had his shorts off in a flash and she sucked in a breath. His cock strut proud and firm, she licked her lips and sank to her knees beside the chair.

Dropping the pineapple spear onto his belly, Jimi leaned over him and swept her tongue over his chest, loving the combination of the sticky sweetness and warmth of his flesh. Lower she licked, following the trail of hair. She cradled his balls, he let out a gasp and his cock jumped. She crushed what juice was left onto his sensitive flesh, and it dripped down from the head to puddle at the base.

"Lick it off." Dallas's voice was gravelly and she turned her head to look at him. She moved a little bit, so his penis was between her and him. She didn't want her head to be in the way. She wanted him to see everything she was going to do to him.

"Did you know that pineapple juice makes semen taste sweet?"

He shook his head.

Jimi smiled and held the base of his cock. Its thickness was like the strongest steel in her hands. She stroked up and down. He moaned, the muscles in his neck bulging as he kept his head lifted so he could watch her. Their gazes locked and she reached her tongue out. He held his breath. She touched the tip of her tongue ever so gently to the tip. Her hair fell down like a curtain, and he grabbed it up into his fist.

"I want to watch you." He growled.

"I want you to watch me," Jimi murmured as her lips pressed the head of his cock.

She leaned her elbow on the chair between his powerful thighs. Taking the pineapple, she placed it against his cock and pressed her lips over the top. She stroked with the pineapple while she sucked on the tip and twirled her tongue around the head. His cock jumped in her hand and she held tighter—increasing her caress on him, tightening and loosening her grip, taking him deeper into her mouth. "Oh, shit." His voice was so deep she hardly recognized it.

He held her hair tighter, and it shot a flash of desire through her. Jimi moaned and increased her cadence on him. She was getting more and more aroused the closer he got to orgasm. His other hand fell on her hip and pulled the sarong aside, his fingers searing a trail down her thigh until he was able to grab her butt, squeezing the cheek in rhythmic movements that matched her gobbling. He slid his fingers down the cleft in her ass, reaching and delicately touching her. The skin he caressed was so unbelievably sensitive she gasped as he pressed his fingers firmer, before sliding away to move his hand between her thighs. Seeking, pressing, finding.

"Mmm." Jimi was getting frantic now, wanting to bring him to orgasm before he did her with his fabulous fingers. Keeping the pump of her hand, she sat up briefly to catch a big breath and focus for a moment on his fingers inside her. Jimi cradled his balls with one hand and stroked with the other, the pineapple now soft in her hand, while she took the head in her mouth. Giving him the ultimate in blow jobs as he finger fucked her.

He groaned and then sucked in a deep breath before blowing it out and thrusting his hips up to her. Jimi was frenzied on him as he brought her to climax. Which made her determined to bring him as much pleasure as he had given her in the shower.

She tried to ignore how skillfully his fingers took her to greater heights and she came fast. Doing her best not to collapse on him with satisfaction, she moaned again when he stilled. He held her head tight on him and let out a roar as he came. Jimi didn't let him come down, though, holding him firmly with her mouth and hands, drawing out his orgasm as long as possible. His body jumped and he gasped. Slowly Jimi released his still-hard cock, cradling him gently, and rested her head on his belly.

"Holy shit," he murmured, and stroked her hair.

"I know," Jimi mumbled next to his belly. She didn't care about the pineapple juice getting in her hair or being sticky. They had that fabulous shower to wash up in. Jimi crawled up beside him on the lounge.

"You have a magic mouth and pineapple hands. Give me a minute, then we can wash off."

"I do try. But then you are very inspiring."

"Well, then, I'm looking forward to seeing what inspires you next time."

14

JIMI PEERED DOWN the pathway leading to the lava tube beyond. She had no idea what to expect, and her claustrophobia niggled in the back of her mind. She tamped it down, though, not wanting it to rise up and take hold. She fought it. No way would she let it ruin this amazing adventure.

After spending the last few days basically living off each other at Dallas's house, they finally ventured back into the world after almost running out of food. Taking this trip up to Volcanoes National Park had been a great idea.

"So, are you brave enough to go inside?"

She chewed her lip and looked across the little bridge that spanned the creek full of lava rock and vegetation. It was very Jurassic Park here and she almost expected a T. rex to come roaring out from the trees.

Steeling herself, she scoffed at him and waved her hand. "Of course I am. Don't be silly."

She didn't realize she'd been wringing her hands to-

gether until he took one in his. Calm flooded through
her and Jimi curled her fingers tightly around his and
held her breath.

He leaned down and whispered, "Come on, you'll
be fine. I'll be here right beside you the whole way."

She drew in a breath and straightened her shoulders
with determination. "Okay. Let's do this."

Jimi stared up at him, looking past his unusual colored
eyes she'd grown to love, deeper, trying to see into his soul,
see what he was really thinking and feeling. She caught
her breath. There was something in there. She knew she
was falling for him with every minute that went by, but he
still seemed to be holding back. Sure, they were fresh and
new. Strangers still. Jimi knew she was letting her mind
run away with all the possibilities. They seemed so good
together. Fit perfectly both physically and, so far, mentally.
So why was she afraid to test the waters, broach the possibility of more time together after this trip?

Now isn't the time. So much was happening so fast
that all her insecurities and trust issues were bubbling to
the surface. She couldn't think about it now. It would take
away from their spontaneity. Something which wasn't
in her nature, but seemed to be making itself known.
She glanced at Dallas—trusting someone else in an uncomfortable situation was hard. Looking into the tunnel ahead, she chewed her lip and then decided he was
worthy of her trust.

She squeezed his hand and drew in a shaky breath.
"Lead the way."

"All righty then."

Stepping along the path shrouded with hanging ferns

and tree branches thick with leaves, they left behind the Hawaiian sunlight as the entrance to the old lava tube yawned before them. It was bigger than she thought. She wasn't sure why she expected it to be small and cramped inside. Maybe this wouldn't be so bad after all. Taking a hesitant step into the tunnel, Jimi looked around in awe when she was inside the entrance. It took a second for her eyes to adjust to the gloom.

"Wow. This is really quite amazing." Lights were strung along the curved wall of the cave, casting an orange glow inside. Water dripped down from the arched and craggy ceiling. Jimi whispered, "I shouldn't have worn flip-flops. Look how uneven and rough the floor is. Puddles everywhere from water dripping." She gripped Dallas's hand tighter. "It's really weird to think that lava flowed through here."

"I know. Makes you realize how small we are in the whole scheme of things. Imagine that below us somewhere is molten lava." Dallas was whispering, too.

"Like, right below us?" Jimi gripped his hand tighter. "Maybe it isn't safe in here."

"It's fine," he assured her.

"Why are we whispering?"

"I don't know—maybe because the other people are whispering, too."

Jimi tilted her head to the side and listened. It was very hushed in the tunnel, and she felt almost a respect for it that called for whispering. It was damp, the humidity seemed high and it was surprisingly cool.

"Watch yourself," Dallas said. "The floor is very uneven, with lots of dips and puddles, and we know how you like to hurt yourself," he teased.

They walked deeper into the tunnel, the people ahead of them disappearing around a curve, and Jimi stopped again.

"Listen," she whispered. "It's so quiet."

Dallas looked behind them. "And we're the only ones in here." He raised up his hands and wiggled his fingers, opening his eyes wide. "Oooh, spooky."

Jimi laughed, and even though she hadn't realized she was feeling tense, his making light of them being alone was helping.

"We can take a walk up there if you like."

Jimi nodded. "I'd like that—if only I hadn't worn such stupid shoes."

Dallas pulled her into his embrace, and she wrapped her arms around his waist and looked up at him. "Don't worry—I can carry you if need be," he assured her.

She smiled and tipped her face up, pursing her lips for a kiss. He didn't disappoint her. She loved his kisses. Right where they stood, in the ancient lava tube where a long time ago thick hot lava had flowed from the volcano down to the ocean, he kissed her. He held her tight, and tongues meshing and sighing into each other, they tasted each other, lost in themselves, until they heard voices of more people entering the lava tube.

Dallas whispered against her lips, "Well, then, I guess that's the signal to move along."

"I guess so." She sighed.

He nudged her forward and she led the way. With him close behind and his fingers resting lightly on her hip, Jimi felt the heat of him behind her. It was so tangible in the damp coolness of the cave she was no longer cool.

They approached a curve in the tunnel.

"I see some light ahead." Jimi looked behind them. The other people were back a ways. Carefully walking over the uneven ground inside the tunnel, they emerged into the light of day. It almost felt different, though, as if something happened to them back in the cave. She had the feel of a new beginning. She was beginning to get clarity on her life and how she'd distanced herself from her origins. Who she was hidden behind an armor of clothes and makeup. She glanced down at herself and realized how far she'd come. She pushed some wayward curls out of her eyes and smiled. Maybe curls weren't so bad after all.

"So what did you think?" Dallas asked. "Was it scary?"

"No, not at all. I was silly for even worrying about it."

Dallas checked his watch. "Hmm, it's getting late. Are you hungry?"

"Yes, a bit. What did you have in mind?"

"Well, I have to run over to the ranch and wondered if you'd like to come with me. Or I could drop you back at the hotel?"

Jimi was a little surprised with this news. She'd almost forgotten he had a life besides being with her. It was very self-centered of her to think of having him all to herself.

"I don't know. Do you drive past the hotel?"

He shook his head. "No, we don't go that way. But it's no problem to drop you off."

They walked back through the overhanging trees, and Jimi thought about it. She wasn't sure about going even though she'd like to. It was weird, wasn't it? To go to his place of employment with him?

"How long would you be? I don't want to be a bother or intrude."

"Don't worry—you wouldn't be intruding or a bother. It's just that I've been away for a couple days and I need to touch base."

"Well, if you think it's okay for me to come, then sure. It'll be different to see it without the pounding rain and driving hurricane." She smiled at him. Plus, she wasn't ready to say goodbye to him just yet.

"It's really hard to believe that storm actually happened."

He held aside a branch and guided her through the narrow opening through the brush.

He's such a gentleman, too. So much about him I adore.

"I'm not sure taking a walk down that path is a good idea. It's starting to get dark. Plus, you have the wrong kind of shoes on."

Jimi looked up and realized he was right. The sky was starting to darken with what looked like storm clouds coming in and the approach of sunset.

"If you think that's best. We're not getting another hurricane, are we?"

He looked up as if reading the sky. "Nah, but I think we're in for some rain. It's a treacherous path, and not wise to do if it's going to get dark or rain."

The little parking lot only had a couple of cars and his truck. He held the door for her and helped her up before slamming the door shut. She watched him walk around and could see he had something on his mind. Her belly did a little flip with trepidation, and she wondered what had made him seem pensive all of a sudden. He climbed in beside her, started the car and grabbed the steering wheel. "This was a great day. It had been a long time since I'd been up here and I'm glad we came. I was happy to show you a bit of our island."

"I loved it. Thank you for driving me around."

Lightning flashed overhead and Jimi sucked in a breath.

"Tell me about your mom." His voice was gentle and encouraging.

"When I was a kid, a weird storm blew in through the night." She took a breath and hesitated.

"And...a storm blew in. They happen. It's nature." His voice was gentle, comforting, and made telling the tragedy a little bit easier.

"My mom died, though." Jimi looked at him, blowing out a puff of breath, and cringed when another bright flash of light lit the darkening sky. Thunder seemed to crash right on top of them.

He raised his eyebrows, then turned back to concentrate on the road and was silent, but she liked how he reached across the console and took her hand. Jimi clutched it, thinking of that horrible night. His fingers stroked with a reassuring motion, and she relaxed a little bit.

"What happened?"

"It's so stupid. We all stayed in bed, and Dad was in another house while she ran around shutting the windows." Jimi swallowed. "She'd gone out on the deck to lower the umbrella, of all things! And lightning struck it, killing her."

"Holy shit."

"Yeah, right? Why would she do such a dumb thing? And why would lightning hit the umbrella and not the tree so close by. It's supposed to strike trees, right? Why her?" Jimi's throat tightened and she didn't want to cry! "If we hadn't lived in the country, out in the boonies, or if Dad wasn't banging another woman, then maybe she wouldn't have died."

"As hard as it may seem, when your time is up your time is up. And that's why you must live in the moment."

Jimi stared at him as he watched the road. He turned to her quickly and her belly tumbled over. Those unique and expressive eyes that captured her in so many ways expressed concern. What a simple explanation. "But I want her back." She sniffed and was so overcome that the tears flowed. "I was eleven, and even fifteen years later I still can't bear it."

"You only have one mom. Of course you miss her." His thumb brushed a tear from her cheek and Jimi leaned into his hand. "And that is why you are afraid of storms."

She nodded. "My dad wasn't there for her. He wasn't even in the house. She tried so hard to please him and she never could. I hate him and the commune way of life for that."

"Honor her memory by overcoming storms, then, and remember all the good things about her."

Jimi nodded. Her heart swelled and she actually felt lighter, like a load had been lifted—the anguish and pain she'd kept buried and hidden and not really acknowledged was there. This wonderful man had said only a few words that seemed to lift the pall that she'd been under for so long. "Th-thank you."

"My pleasure. You mentioned once 'all the children.' Do you have siblings?"

She nodded. "Not all from the same mother, though. I was her only." She peered out the window, glad he didn't ask her to elaborate that point because she was pretty sure he understood the whole *free love* thing.

They fell into a comfortable silence as they drove along the highway. Until his phone rang. He dug it out of his pocket, which totally reminded Jimi that she should get back to her hotel room, too. She had a business back home that she needed to check in on. What if something had happened since she'd been gone and didn't know? Now she was starting to worry about a little bit of everything.

"Aloha."

Jimi smiled at his island greeting to the person on the other end of the line. But didn't want to eavesdrop on the one-sided conversation, so she looked out the window of the truck as he drove back the way they had come a little while ago.

"Yes. On my way. I won't be long now. How's the foal?" He sighed, and Jimi looked at him. He was nodding at what was being said to him on the other end of the line. Then his face went hard and a muscle jumped in his cheek. "What? No, of course not." He paused and listened. "No, not interested. Look, okay, I know. I said I'd be there soon."

Jimi bit her lip, hearing the agitation in his voice. She was starting to super worry now. What was all that about? She had a bad feeling all of a sudden.

DALLAS DID HIS best not to show how pissed off he was. That phone call from Larson was not what he wanted to hear. He glanced over at Jimi, and anxiety started to fill him. What the hell was going to happen now? He gripped the steering wheel and twisted his hands on it. He hadn't thought about Selena in years. Larson was all wound up over the fact Selena was back and threatening to show up at the ranch. Just what she was thinking was beyond him. He shook his head and blew out a puff of air, not wanting any kind of confrontation with his ex.

Jimi moved on the seat next to him. He looked at her and gritted his teeth when he saw the worried expression on her face. He didn't have a clue what to say to her about this.

"Is everything okay?"

He nodded, and answered in a low voice, "Nothing I can't handle." He grimaced, realizing he sounded more angry than he'd really wanted to let on.

"That sounds rather dire."

He shook his head and stretched his arms out so they were straight on the steering wheel and drew in a deep breath.

"Nope. Not dire. Everything will be fine." Dallas

reached across the truck console and took her hand, squeezing her fingers.

He wasn't ready to tell her everything yet. The fact that he hadn't told her earlier was only because he didn't know the direction they were going in. He'd been hurt once before, jilted at the altar. Plus, it hurt too much to dredge up the past. But now with Selena back after all these years and telling Larson she was planning on coming over to the ranch, it made him think fast and hard about a future with Jimi. If a girl who was used to the ranch life like Selena had been able to run away from it and live on the mainland, how could a main-lander ever consider island life?

He sighed, wondering what would bring Selena back after all these years. He'd heard tidbits of information about her now and again. It seemed they were all so quick to tell him what she was up to whenever news leaked back to the island. He'd loved her and thought she was the love of his life. And now she was back.

"You know, you can always take me back to the hotel. If you have something to deal with, it might be best." Jimi's voice interrupted his thoughts.

"No, I want you to come back to the ranch. I don't have anything to deal with right now. It's all good and I'd really like you with me."

"Only if you're sure."

"I'm sure."

15

JIMI FELT A little ill at ease though Dallas was trying to make her feel better. She had a deep sense of foreboding. Even the darkening skies as they drove closer to the ranch seemed to foretell the developing mood.

When he pulled up in front of the big ranch house she was a little bit surprised, fully expecting to go to the barn or the bunkhouse. So she was slightly confused when they walked up the nice, wide stairs onto the wraparound porch.

"This is a lovely house." The rag rugs and the rocking chairs with colorful Western-decor pillows gave the feeling they were in the Wild West, not here in tropical Hawaii. The only indication of that were the gorgeous flowers climbing along the deck railing.

"Thank you. We love it."

Jimi furrowed her brows. Why would he thank her for liking a house that wasn't his and say "we" love it? When he walked up to the front door, opened it and stepped inside without knocking or announcing their arrival, it truly confounded her. He behaved like this was his house.

But he has a house, on a cliff.

"Come on, let's grab a drink and find out where everybody is." He took her hand and led her into a spectacular room with floor-to-ceiling windows along the far wall. They looked out across rolling meadows and down to the sea in the distance. Jimi was awestruck.

She shook her head, still unable to process what was happening here.

"Everybody? Dallas, I'm confused. I thought when you said we'd go to the ranch it would be to the barn or somewhere else, not to the main house. Is it okay to be in here?"

"What do you mean, is it okay to be in here? Of course it is."

"Is it okay with the owners?"

He had a perplexed look on his face. "What? This is my house. We are the owners."

Jimi stopped in her tracks, and because she was holding on to Dallas's hand, he stopped, also. "Hang on a minute. Are you telling me you own this ranch?"

"I thought that was obvious." He said it rather hesitantly, looking at her with a concerned expression. "Is there something wrong with that?"

Jimi blinked and tried to process this new information. It had never dawned on her he owned the ranch, only that he worked on it. As an employee here.

"N-no, nothing wrong with that and, no, it never occurred to me. It's just that nothing over the past week or so gave me any indication otherwise. You never said anything. Why?"

He shrugged and looked as if he was trying to come up with something to say. "Well, I didn't think I needed to. I figured it was obvious."

She fanned her hand back and forth as if it would help her understand what she was hearing here. "Well, I kind of think it was important. I get the feeling now that you were hiding it from me. Why? Did you think I was a gold digger?"

He shifted on his feet and looked uncomfortable. "No. I never thought that, and actually I'm a little offended by it."

"Well, I'm offended that you wouldn't tell me. I feel like you've been keeping me in the dark. It makes me feel kind of foolish now." She put her hands on her hips. "And who's *we*?"

He stepped forward and held her shoulders. Jimi looked up into his eyes, and seeing the look of concern relieved her own sense of unease a little bit.

"Honestly, I figured you knew right from the beginning. And I don't think you are a gold digger." He paused and pressed a kiss to her lips. "And the *we* is my brother and sister. Tucker and Larson. Who you've met."

"Oh." Jimi looked up into his eyes, trying to read them and determine if he was being truthful or not. Nothing in them gave her any indication otherwise. Plus, if she thought back over the last days with him, he didn't seem to have deliberately held anything back—they just had never talked about it. She hadn't talked much about her life, either, so how could she judge him? "I guess we have a lot to talk about, don't we?"

Dallas nodded. "Something to look forward to." He smiled and took her hand. "Come on, I'd like to officially introduce you to my brother and sister."

"I'd like that." She smiled back and followed him through the magnificent rooms. The closer they got to the kitchen, the louder the voices in there became. Some even sounded a little bit angry. Nerves filled her belly and she held Dallas's hand tighter.

"Don't worry—they're not going to eat you up. They're likely having a wild and crazy argument with some friends." He leaned down and whispered in her ear, "I'm saving the eating part for me later."

She laughed and gave him a swat on the shoulder. "Timing, cowboy, timing. Not a good thing to have me blushing in front of your brother and sister."

The kitchen was fantastic. A big country kitchen all done in natural wood tones with white and deep blue accents. More windows graced the far wall, and beyond the cooking area was a big, wide island surrounded by a group of people. Beer and wine bottles were scattered on the surface, as well as bags of chips and pretzels. Jimi tried to assess the mood of everyone around the island. When Dallas made an odd low hissing sound and pulled up short, her heart dropped.

All faces turned to them and silence filled the room. She felt profoundly uncomfortable and made sure she stayed rooted to the spot beside Dallas, even though she felt like hiding behind him. She recognized a couple of faces from the camp—his brother and another man.

One woman was sitting down, and she recognized her as the one who'd given her the bad news about her suitcase. Jimi's heart dropped, remembering how uptight she'd been that day. Even a little short-tempered, and, of course, that had been with his sister. Great start and first impressions. Another woman was standing off to the side a bit, her purse strap still slung over her shoulder, like she'd just arrived.

It wasn't difficult to pick up the nervous glance Larson swung between the woman and Dallas. Jimi scanned the faces of the other people and she saw they also held strange expressions. The silence lingered and Jimi looked at Dallas. His face was thunderous. She'd never seen him so angry before. The muscles in his jaw twitched, and his temple even seemed to pulse. His face was darkening and Jimi widened her eyes with surprise. This was a new Dallas to her.

"Dallas?" she whispered. "What's happening here?"

He didn't answer her and continued to stare at the other people. And then she noticed his gaze switch over to the woman. All the emotions that ran across his face made it like an open book and Jimi gasped. Instinctively, she knew he'd loved this woman at one point in time. And it looked as if he still might. She dropped his hand and stepped away from him, the sense of doom she'd had earlier crashing down around her. It was like he'd forgotten she was there, so intent on the woman across the room.

Jimi looked at her. The woman was intensely focused on Dallas. She was dark haired and dark eyed, but when she walked around the center island toward Dallas, Jimi caught the full impact of her voluptuous beauty. Clearly she had Hawaiian blood. Her thick hair fell to her slender waist, and her body was so perfect Jimi bet she was a hula dancer. She could imagine her dancing with graceful and seductive movements.

Tucker, Larson and the other people glanced back and forth between Dallas and the woman. Jimi was all but forgotten and rather glad of it. She took a step back as if to get ready to bolt from the room and back out the door she'd just come through.

"Dallas." The woman spoke, and it sounded like musical notes. Suddenly Jimi wished she was properly made-up, her hair done just so and wearing designer clothes. Not in the newly bought shorts and tank top, her bare feet in flip-flops and, surely, her hair a wild riot around her head. She raised her hand to smooth her hair back into place. Jimi felt the need to have her armor around her because without it right now, she felt like nothing.

Maybe that was why she'd hidden behind the makeup and the clothes all these years. She'd never felt good enough. Until last week, after meeting Dallas. But now, seeing him so focused on this gorgeous, natural beauty, totally forgetting Jimi was even in the same room with him, made her question everything, including their last few days together.

"Selena, what are you doing here?" Dallas's voice was ice.

"I've come here to see you. I've missed you, Dallas."

She walked toward him, flicking her gaze over to Jimi as if noticing her for the first time. The look on the woman's face told Jimi all she needed to know. She'd come for Dallas. And she was determined to get Dallas. Her dark gaze slid away from Jimi and back to Dallas.

Tears sprang to Jimi's eyes. In those few brief seconds came the crashing realization that she was falling in love with him. Hard. And on the heels of that was knowing she was going to lose him before she ever had a chance to get him. How could she ever compete with an ex? And a stunningly beautiful one at that.

Silence filled the kitchen. The tension was thick and Jimi wasn't sure what to do. She wanted to flee. Run away. But something held her rooted to the spot. Selena stepped closer to Dallas, and Jimi watched to see his reaction. He stiffened and tipped his head back slightly. His hands were balled into fists.

"Dallas," Selena said softly, "it's good to see you. Can we go somewhere and talk?"

He didn't say anything. And Jimi willed him to tell this woman to go back to wherever it was she'd come from. But he didn't. He stayed silent and watched Selena. His face was a myriad of emotions until it finally settled down into an expression she was unable to read. The other woman stepped closer until they were about a foot apart. She looked up into his face and Dallas looked down at her.

Jimi covered her mouth, just in case the sob she felt bubbling up inside rushed out. She quickly glanced over at the table, to see everyone else sitting around with their eyes wide and mouths like surprised O's. Clearly, whatever was going on here was a big deal. What had been the relationship between these two? Just as Jimi was about to step forward and take Dallas's hand in hers, he reached out to Selena. Jimi froze and held her breath.

"Selena." He spoke her name in a soft tone, but Jimi heard the hard edge, and it gave her a sense of hope, even more so when he dropped his head and shoved his hands in his jeans pockets. "There really isn't anything to say."

"Come on, Dallas. Of course we have lots to talk about." Her voice sounded whiny, like a spoiled child. "Can we please talk in private?"

"Why? What good will it do?" He took a step back and toward Jimi, but he kept his hands in his pockets.

Selena didn't miss the movement and shot a quick glance at Jimi, perhaps realizing for the first time that she was here with Dallas.

"Who's your friend?" The look that Selena gave Jimi was caustic.

But in that moment, Jimi decided she wasn't going to let this woman make her feel unworthy, regardless of whatever kind of past Dallas had with her. Everyone had pasts and it was how you dealt with the present that showed true strength.

Jimi stepped toward Dallas and reached out, sliding her hand down his forearm. She gently tugged his hand from his pocket and laced his fingers with hers. Relief flooded through her, unlike anything she'd ever felt before. This was huge. His actions clearly stated *something* for this woman to understand.

"Anything you want to say, Selena, can be said here in front of friends and family." Dallas let go of Jimi's hand and wrapped it around her shoulder, pulling her tight against him. "Our past is done, Selena." Dallas's voice brooked no room for argument.

Selena's face darkened. The beauty Jimi had seen in her a few moments ago was replaced by ugliness and pain, and for the briefest moment she almost felt sorry for this woman.

"How can it be? We're engaged. We were going to get married!"

"Yes, we were. Until you took off right before the wedding."

"You're engaged to be married? And to her?" Jimi couldn't be more surprised, another thing he hadn't told her. How many more secrets did he have?

For the first time since entering the kitchen, Dallas turned to Jimi. The stern expression he'd had when staring at Selena softened when he looked at her. He sighed, and she felt the stiffness of his body relax as he focused on her.

"No, we are not engaged. We were, but that was eight years ago. Everything was planned, everything was arranged, and yes, I did love her." He drew in a breath. "Not anymore."

"Tell me," Jimi whispered and nodded. "It's okay. I need to know." She was dying to see the expression on Selena's face, but she kept her attention fully on Dallas. A connection he needed if he was going to tell her anything.

"She wanted me to leave the island. Because she wanted more than could be offered here. More than I can offer her. So she left the morning of our wedding without a word."

This time Jimi looked over at Selena and then back to Dallas. "How horrible. I'm so sorry. But if you still have feelings for her and need to… I understand." Jimi's heart was breaking into a thousand pieces. She had no idea what he was going to say and was almost overcome by how upset she was getting.

"Dallas, she's right. I know you still have feelings for me. I'm sorry I didn't respond to you when you tried to find me, but I just couldn't come back."

"So why *are* you back? You found your rich man on the mainland. Which was all you wanted in the end anyways…the money."

She shook her head, panic etched on her face. "No, I came back for you. I know you love me and I'm sorry I left. I should never have done that. We can try again."

Larson gasped from the other side of the room and Jimi glanced at her. She had slid off the stool and stood up, rounding the island as if about to do battle. But with whom?

"Dallas, what are you thinking?" Larson took a few more steps forward.

He held up his hand and his sister stopped in her tracks. Then he turned his gaze onto Selena. Jimi nearly burst into tears of relief when he pulled her tighter and wrapped his arm around her shoulder even more possessively than before. The icing on the cake was when he leaned down and kissed her temple.

It's going to be fine. He's fine. It'll be fine.

"Selena, I said before there's nothing to discuss. We are ancient history. I have no feelings for you whatsoever. The love I did feel for you once is long gone. After you left, I heard you got married. So likely he dropped you and now you're coming back to see what you can get from me. But I am not an old bone you can dig up from the dirt and chew again."

He walked around Selena toward Larson, Tucker and the others sitting around the center island still with stupefied expressions on their faces.

"Guys, I'd like to introduce you to Jimi. The new woman in my life."

"The new woman in your life?" Selena's voice shushed them all, and Dallas turned to her.

"Yes. It's time for you to leave. Now." He strode to the door and held it open. "This is the last time I'll ever hold the door open for you again. The only reason I am right now is because I can shut it behind you."

Selena stood for a moment, uncertainty clear on her face. Then she huffed and yanked on her purse strap. "All I can say is, thank God I didn't marry you. The best thing I ever did was walk out on you or I'd be stuck with you crazy-assed people. Bunch of hillbillies." And she flounced out the door, leaving everyone in stunned silence.

"Well, that was a fucking gong show," Tucker said, which sent everyone into gales of laughter. "Who needs a drink?"

"I know I do," Jimi answered, and took a stool at the island.

"What's your pleasure?" Tucker asked her.

"Got any bourbon?" She smiled.

Tucker laughed. "My kind of woman."

"Just one that needs her nerves calmed down."

Larson spoke up first. "Okay, okay, this has been a slice, but explain please? Forget about that one." She pointed at the closed door. "How long have you known Jimi, and where did you meet her?"

This time Jimi decided to ease the burden off Dallas. Her heart was smiling with love for him, and she knew now she wanted to try to work on a future together. She was going to do everything she could to make it right.

"First, Larson, I need to apologize to you for my behavior last week at the camp." Jimi slipped off the stool and walked around to Larson and put out her hand. "I was not my best last week when I arrived for the wedding—"

"Oh, now I remember you!" Larson exclaimed. "Your suitcase, thinking you were in the wrong place." She cast a glance at Dallas and then gave him a sly smile. "Oh, I get it. Somehow you guys hooked up during the wedding fiasco."

He broke out in a wide grin. Everyone seemed to breathe a sigh of relief, and instantly the tension in the room dissipated. "Guilty as charged."

"I wondered about that," Tucker announced. "You guys are pretty sneaky. But when I look back now, I can see it. We were just all too blind under the circumstances. What's the goddamn secret anyways?"

Dallas shrugged his shoulders. "No secret. Just nobody's business."

"So, Jimi—" Larson sat down across from her "—tell us a little bit about you."

Tucker put the tumbler in front of her and she took a long drink, loving the fiery burn as the liquid settled in her stomach. She was reminded of just how empty it was, so she pulled over a bag of chips and took a few.

The weight of Dallas's hand when he squeezed her shoulder was welcome and matched the sizzle from the bourbon. She was warming up in more ways than one and shifted a bit on the stool. She looked up at him, giving him a smile that he returned. This time she saw more emotion in his eyes than ever before. Her heart swelled for this man, and she couldn't wait until they were alone to talk... And more.

"You know what," he said, "why don't we just chill for a little while. We can have a chat later. We just came up for a quick visit here to discuss a couple of business items. Let's get this meeting done with so I can get Jimi back down to her hotel."

"I'm in no rush," Jimi interjected. "I'm enjoying this drink." She relaxed on the stool, sipping the bourbon.

"Not often a woman is a bourbon drinker," Tucker complimented. "Bottoms up."

He raised his glass and Jimi clinked hers with his. They both shot what was left in their glasses.

"So this is a new side to you," Dallas commented before taking a deep swig of his beer.

Jimi smiled and murmured, "I guess there's a lot we don't know about each other, isn't there?"

He nodded and put the beer bottle down. "Apparently." Then he gave her a cheeky grin. "Discovery can be the most exciting part."

"Okay, how about we leave all that discovery stuff for another time? Preferably when you're alone...and not in a group setting?" Tucker suggested, and they all laughed, which helped to ease the lingering tension in the kitchen.

"Right then, since you both are here, as well." Dallas nodded at the two guys in full cowboy gear across the island. "Jimi, these rascals are the lead wranglers. You might remember John from the camp. And this big bruiser here is Rourke. He's family, of the blood kind. Came down to be a *paniolo* for a while from our spread in Wyoming."

"You have another ranch in Wyoming?"

Dallas nodded.

"Texas, too," Rourke added as he stood up. "I much prefer here and Texas over Wyoming any day. Warmth, sun and surfing."

Surfing?

"Really, you surf? That just seems, um…" How could she say it without insulting him? So she let the thought trail away.

"Unexpected?" Rourke finished her thought. "Yeah, I'm big, but I ain't no barney and can ride in the drop."

Jimi blinked. What had he just said? She couldn't get over the size of him. He towered over everyone and was a younger version of the actor Sam Elliott. He had the kindest and bluest eyes she'd ever seen, but they also held a mischievous glint in them.

"A'A, Jimi." He emphasized the first *A*, Ah-ha, then leaned closer to her and whispered, "A Hawaiian greeting."

"Ooh, I see. A'A, Rourke." Jimi took his outstretched hand. "You're speaking a foreign language!"

With his other one, he swept off his cowboy hat and

nodded his head, his long blond hair falling over his tanned face. "Ma'am, pleasure to meet ya." His cowboy drawl was charming, and completely opposite to what must have been surfer lingo.

"What's 'barney'?" she asked him.

His bright smile was infectious, and she found herself smiling right along with him. "An inexperienced surfer, *wahine.*"

Her eyebrows shot up. *"Wahine?"*

"Yeah, *wahine* is *girl.* I think you could be a surfer girl. Don't you?"

"Ahh, I don't know." Jimi cast a glance at Dallas, who was standing there with an equally big grin on his face and his arms crossed over his chest.

"Up to you, *hemahema.*"

"Nooo!" Rourke shouted. "She's not!"

"I'm afraid she is," Dallas answered him, humor ringing in his voice.

Jimi was perplexed and then remembered. "I am not clumsy. I could surf. If I wanted to."

"Just teasing you, *wahine,*" Rourke said.

"Now, boys," Larson cut in. "I think there's been enough drama for one day. So I have an idea. The meeting can be put off for a few days. That way these lovebirds can get back on their getting-to-know-you schedule."

Murmurs of agreement to Larson's suggestion were silenced by Jimi. "Please, don't change your plans because of me. I understand business takes priority." Jimi stood and held out her glass to Tucker. "How about you top me up, and I'll make myself scarce for a while." She could see Dallas was about to argue back. "No, really,

Dallas, it's fine. See—" she held up the tumbler "—full glass, and I'll find something to do until you've had your meeting."

Jimi lifted to her toes and gave him a kiss.

"Ooh, look at that," Tucker teased. "Love is in the air, Dallas. Soon we'll be planning your nuptials."

"Now, don't get ahead of yourself there. Who said anything about marriage? We still have to get to know each other." He glanced at her. "On that note, catch you later."

She left through the same door Selena had, and wandered down the porch steps. Her thoughts weighed heavily, especially after Dallas's resistance to the suggestion of marriage. He'd obviously been burned once. Did that mean forever? She wanted to try to make *something* work for them. And now she wasn't sure that was what he would want.

16

"Looks like you might have a little explaining to do, yourself," Dallas said, when she led him up the steps to her suite at the Four Seasons.

"What do you mean?"

"I'm pretty sure that you need to have some kind of financial freedom in order to afford one of the top suites at this resort."

She smiled and answered, "Do you think so?"

He nodded and followed her into the suite after she pushed the door open. Dallas whistled. "Impressive. I've never been in one of these suites before, let alone any of the rooms. But I heard they're very nice. And now I can say for myself, they are."

Dallas wandered over to the windows overlooking the deck, beach and ocean. He unlocked and pushed them open.

"Not quite the same view as from my place, but still pretty spectacular."

"No, it's not," Jimi replied, as she came up and

wrapped her arm around his waist. "I adore this view, but I certainly love yours, as well."

He walked out onto the deck, bringing her with him. He let out a big sigh, glad the drama at the ranch earlier was over and done with. Dallas wondered if Jimi could ever see herself living on his ranch, his pride and joy. With him. He knew she had a successful business practically on the other side of the world. He blew out a heavy breath.

"What?" Jimi asked.

"I was just thinking about everything."

"Everything?"

He laughed and stepped out of her embrace, wandering over to the railing to gaze across the waves. He breathed in the ocean air, liking how it rejuvenated him. He felt good. And a little worried.

"She was years ago. And, yeah, she broke my heart pretty bad by taking off before the wedding. But she did me a big favor—just like I said to her. If I'd married her, it would have likely ended up in a divorce."

"She is beautiful."

"I won't deny that," Dallas agreed, "but the beauty was only skin-deep." He turned and took her shoulders in his hands. "Unlike you. Your beauty is not only skin-deep, it goes right down into your soul. The way you handled yourself back there was classic grace."

Jimi looked up at him, and he fell into the softness of her eyes. She was his haven. A safe place. The way she gazed up at him, the open honesty on her face, gave Dallas a bit more assurance.

"I don't know what to say," Jimi whispered.

Dallas could see her confusion, as well. He wanted to alleviate any concerns she might have. "That's okay—not everything can be said with words. Actions speak louder. And your actions back at the ranch came through to me loud and clear. I like you in my life, Jimi."

"Your life? How so?" Her voice grew softer, and Dallas pulled her into a tight hug.

"I want to get to know you. Who you are and, yes, your commune days, too."

They both laughed at that.

"I'm pretty much an open book, Dallas. The last days with you have been a whirlwind, just like when we first met. There's been so much drama around us, complications and craziness, that we've only really had private time at your cliff house. We haven't even started to scratch the surface of what our lives were like before each other."

"I know," Dallas agreed. "We have a lot to learn about each other. After what happened today, I feel like it was a pretty big step in the right direction."

"Me, too. I'd like to tell you a little more about me, as well. This—" Jimi waved her hand back toward the hotel suite behind them "—and how I can do it. Yes, I have my own business in New York City. A high-fashion design house and it's doing very well. Well enough to afford this and other luxuries. I don't want to ever forget my childhood, and it had its challenges, trust me. But now isn't the time to get into all that."

She took a breath. "What I do want you to know is my time with you has given me a new outlook on life. I no longer feel the need to shield myself behind clothes and makeup, like when I first arrived and all those years before meeting you. You accepted me for who I was, disheveled, in borrowed clothes. And you have no idea how special that is for me."

"That's what I love about you. The way you were able to roll with the complications put in front of you. And with no complaints."

Dallas heard the word *love* fall out of his mouth and he watched her carefully to see if her facial expression indicated she'd heard it, as well. He saw her eyes light up a little bit, and then her lips curved into a sweet smile. His heart welled with emotion. An unfamiliar feeling, so different from what he'd felt as a young man when he thought he was in love. Did he even dare to entertain the idea of marriage again? Of love? But if what he was feeling now was any indication, he'd better accept that it was entirely possible.

"It certainly was a growing experience for me. Strangely, I'm really glad everything happened the way it did. Otherwise, I would never have found you." The honesty he heard in her voice affected him deeply.

"And me. Had none of this happened, you wouldn't have come into my life and showed me that there is hope."

Jimi wound her arms around his neck. He tipped his head back, liking how her fingers thrust into his hair. She pulled his head down and Dallas stopped a hairbreadth from her. The air between them crackled to life, and his body reacted in a way that wasn't only sexual, it was with a deep desire to claim her as his own. She looked up at him with her wonderful eyes.

Dallas groaned, overcome with emotion. He crushed her mouth under his, running his tongue along her lips until she opened for him.

The way she moaned into him was more than he could resist. He swept her into his arms, taking her back through the living room.

"In there," Jimi murmured next to his mouth. She pointed to the door off to the left.

She knew exactly where he wanted to go. The bedroom.

Setting her on the large bed, Dallas leaned over her. "Now, for the first time since we met, I'm going to make love to you properly."

"You've always done it properly."

He took a scarf sitting in a heap on the bedside table and covered her eyes. Lifting her head gently so he didn't catch her hair, Dallas secured it so it wouldn't slip off.

"No, I mean like this."

JIMI LAY ON the bed, trembling. This man did it all to her. And in all the right ways. He hadn't even touched her other than covering her eyes and she was a quivering, panting mess. His hands, gentle yet firm and warm, traced the path over her cheeks and down her neck. She moaned as he moved farther down, and goose bumps rose along her flesh. She felt her nipples rise up into aching points, desperate for his touch. Squirming under his stroking only made them rub more deliciously against her top.

His hands stopped at her waist and, circling it, gently pushed her top up. The sensation of being blindfolded and the mystery of his touch had her turned on to a fever pitch. She couldn't lie still, and she tried to sit up.

"No, *ho'onanea*. Let me."

"Wh-what does that mean again... I can't remember. Ooh."

"Relax. Lift your arms up."

She did as she was told. The whoosh of fabric over her arms meant she was bare to him now.

"You are so beautiful. I can't get enough of looking at you. Tasting you."

A warm wetness sealed around her nipple and Jimi cried out in sheer delight as desire fanned over her body and straight down to her pussy. She ached for him to fill her and squeezed her thighs together, restless on the bed as his lips suckled her and his tongue rasped across her nipple.

"Oh, Dallas, don't make me wait for you."

Coolness washed over the nipple he'd just given such sweet attention to as he moved across her chest. "Mustn't forget this one."

Jimi moaned and shoved at her shorts, desperate to get them off. Dallas pushed her hands away and ran his palms down her hips, taking her shorts with them until she felt them pulled off over her feet. He touched her ankles and slid his hands higher, past her knees, to her thighs. Gently pushing them apart. Jimi melted. Knowing he was looking at her nakedness—but unable to see what he was doing—and hearing his hitched breathing was one of the most erotic moments of her life.

The blindfold disappeared and she blinked in surprise. He reared above her, magnificent, his eyes full of his desire and hair wild about his head. She gasped, unable to believe such a gorgeous man was here with her. She knew she would never tire of looking at him, his dark ruffled hair that rested against his neck, wide shoulders and unbelievably muscled chest and arms. She wanted to touch the whisper of hair on his chest and reached for him. Pressing her hands on his muscled belly, she closed her eyes as desire raced through her. She slid them up as far as she could reach.

He took hold of her hands with his and wrapped the scarf around them.

"What are you doing?" she asked, breathless.

"Tying you up." He looked at her and she drew in a shaky breath when he asked her, "Is that okay?"

She nodded frantically. "I think so, yes. I've never been tied up before."

"It's just your hands, and it's loose—so if you want to pull them free, you can."

"I—I won't," she whispered, and shook her head. She gasped when he pulled her hands up and tied them to the headboard. Jimi had never felt so helpless yet so wonderfully empowered. She gave up her control to him because being bound by him, lying under him with him in charge, was so terribly exciting, and it felt glorious.

When he dropped his gaze, she followed and saw what he was doing. Holding his cock in his hand, he slowly sheathed himself, rolling the condom down. Seeing his hands on his cock ramped up her arousal. Jimi was so ready for him. When he looked at her, she held her breath.

"Did you like that? Watching me?"

She nodded, unable to form coherent words.

"Good."

His weight pressed down on the bed as he settled between her thighs. His cock, hard and impatient, jutted toward her. Just as impatient as she was to feel him in her. He leaned over her, running his tongue from her belly button along her hypersensitive skin to suck on each hardened nipple. She pulled on the scarf, desperately needing to touch him. But she didn't want to be untied, so she lay still.

"That's it. Close your eyes…feel. Clear your mind and let your body speak to you as it does to me."

She looked at him as he spoke, next to her breast, before flicking his tongue over her nipple. Jimi moaned and closed her eyes, focusing on his touch. When she felt his cock at her opening, she drew in a breath and waited, lifting her hips. He pressed into her, and she sighed, a long, low sigh of ecstasy. Deep, slow and delicious. She raised her hips to him some more, meeting him, and their cadence began. His hand slid across her belly and down to her clit, where he swirled his finger in time with his thrusts.

"O-oh, Dallas. Don't…stop. *So* good."

He groaned and gritted his teeth. His sex sounds were so exciting to her, and she felt her orgasm build. Holding her breath, she tightened her legs around him, grinding against him so his hand was wonderfully trapped between them.

Then it was on her. She sucked in a deep breath, suspended for that achingly sweet moment before her climax crashed through her body. Dallas loosened her hands and she wrapped her arms around him. As he did her, his face buried into her neck as he rolled them over until she was on top.

Jimi arched her back and rocked her hips on him. His hands grasped her breasts, plucking at her nipples. She was going to come again! She felt him swell and fill her, exciting her already tingling nerve endings to new life. Another orgasm swept through her and she couldn't stay upright, falling over him. He bucked his hips and pulled her down on him, holding her in place as he groaned, coming in great pulsing throbs deep inside her.

Multiple!

This man was a miracle and she hugged him as if never to let him go. Slowly they quieted. She rested on him, not moving for what seemed an eternity, before rolling to the side. He stretched out on his back.

Jimi moved onto her side, propped up her head on one hand and placed the other on his belly. It quivered beneath her touch and she smiled at how the tables had turned now. His control over, hers just beginning. He turned his head and looked at her. The smile on his face was that of a contented man.

"Happy?" she asked him.

"Never more so," he answered.

Jimi dropped her head to the pillow and they stared at each other in comfortable silence for a few minutes as they both caught their breath.

A few moments later, Jimi stood and grabbed a pareo on the chair, tying it around her. She walked to the window, feeling his gaze on her the whole time. She pushed the windows aside, and the warm, sweet sea air blew in. A sense of well-being filled her. It was a completely foreign emotion, one that she'd never imagined she'd feel. And all because of the man who had just made love to her.

"Sunset is coming." Jimi watched the sky streak in an array of colors she'd only ever seen in Hawaii. But tonight they seemed so much more vivid.

"We have a thing for sunsets."

She turned to him. "I want to show you something."

"Do I have to get dressed?"

Jimi laughed and stooped to pick up his shorts on the floor, then tossed them to him.

"I think it might be a good idea. Now, hurry. There's not much time."

Dallas bounded from the bed and disappeared into the bathroom. He was back moments later with his shorts on.

Jimi grabbed his hand. "Come on."

She led him onto the deck and down the stairs into the soft sand by the sea.

"Where are we going?"

She pointed up the beach. "There."

They walked through the calm surf as it lapped lazily at their toes and the white sand. Hand in hand. She glanced at him and then back at the setting sun.

"What is this place?" he asked as he helped her up the black lava steps.

"Isn't it lovely? Stand here." She pulled him next to the tree and the outcrop of black lava rock that jutted over the blue water below them. "This is the Wedding

Tree. Where Diana and Matt got married. Where I sat looking for you."

He glanced at the trees arching over them, then out over the water before settling his gaze on her. "You did?"

Jimi nodded. "I did. I was so let down when you didn't come."

"But you know the reason why now?"

"Yes, I do."

"Do you forgive me for not coming, or rather, for being late and not recognizing you?"

"Of course I do. I just wished we hadn't missed each other."

He smiled and she returned it, love blooming in her chest.

"You've just said a whole lot of 'I dos.'"

She nodded. "Yes, I have, haven't I?"

"So how do you think we will make this work?"

"I'm sure we'll think of something." Jimi was breathless with anticipation. What was going to come next? She wasn't silly enough to think this was a proposal, but there was some thought to the future. Right?

"I think I have an idea."

"And that is…?"

"You need to set up shop here, in Hawaii."

She fell silent. She turned and gazed up at him. He looked concerned. Her hesitation had alarmed him and Jimi's heart softened for him. "Dallas, I've thought of that. I'm not sure how it would work, though. I'm finally getting established."

"I understand."

"But that doesn't mean I won't consider it. In fact, it had crossed my mind when you took me to the ladies' shop the other day. So maybe we can start looking at how we could try and make that happen." Her heart burst wide open for him and the joy on his face.

Dallas folded her in his strong embrace, and Jimi melted into him. She tipped her head back, waiting for a kiss. He didn't disappoint, and their lips touched just as the sun kissed the horizon. Their kiss deepened, holding promises as the sinking sun painted the sky. Maybe dreams did come true in blue Hawaii.

* * * * *

SPECIAL EXCERPT FROM

⬦ HARLEQUIN

Blaze

Captain Nolee Arnauyq has never wanted or needed to be rescued. Until her crab fishing boat is caught in a violent storm and gorgeous Coast Guard rescue swimmer Dylan Holt lands on her deck.

Read on for a sneak preview of
HIS LAST DEFENSE,
the latest Karen Rock title from the series
UNIFORMLY HOT!

"We have one minute," he heard his commander say through his helmet's speakers. "Is your captain ready? Over?"

"She will be," Dylan answered. He slung an arm over a rope line and held fast when another swell lifted him off his feet. The ship groaned as sheets of metal strained against each other like fault lines before an earthquake. The lashings clanked. "Send down the strop. Over."

"You have fifty seconds and then I want you on deck, Holt," barked his commander.

Dylan shoved his way along the slick deck, propelling himself across its steep slant. "Roger that."

He would get Nolee out. End of story.

Descending as fast as he dared, he fought the wind and dropped down into the hull again. Icy water made his breath catch even with the benefit of the dry suit. Nolee should have been out of here long before now.

HBEXP0317

"I've almost got it." Her strained voice emerged from blue lips. Her movements were jerky as she twisted wire around the still gushing pipe. She was losing motor function. Hypothermia was already setting in.

"It's over, Nolee. Come with me now."

When she opened her mouth, her head lolled. Her eyelids dropped. Reacting on instinct, he grabbed her limp form before she crumpled into the freezing water.

He hauled her out of the hull and across the deck where a rescue strop dangled. Damn, damn, damn. His hands weren't cooperating, his own motor function feeling the effects of the cold. Once he'd tethered them together, he gave his flight mechanic a thumbs-up. The boat flung them sideways, careening over the rail.

Swinging, their feet skimmed the deadly swells. The line jerked them up through the stinging air. He tightened his arms around her. With only a tether connecting her to him, he couldn't lose his grip.

As they rose, he forced himself not to look at her. He'd dreamed about that face too many times, even after he left Kodiak to forget her.

But he wouldn't be doing his job if he didn't hold her close. And heaven help him—no matter how much she'd gutted him nine years ago—he couldn't deny she felt damned good in his arms.

Don't miss
HIS LAST DEFENSE by Karen Rock,
available April 2017 wherever
Harlequin® Blaze® books and ebooks are sold.

www.Harlequin.com

Turn your love of reading into
rewards you'll love with

Harlequin My Rewards

**Join for FREE today at
www.HarlequinMyRewards.com**

Earn **FREE BOOKS** of your choice.

Experience **EXCLUSIVE OFFERS** and contests.

Enjoy **BOOK RECOMMENDATIONS**
selected just for you.

PLUS! Sign up now
and get **500** points
right away!

Earn **FREE** REWARDS
HarlequinMyRewards.com
Join Today!

MYR16R